One

One Thousand Buddhas But Who's Counting

By

Marie LeClaire

Enjoy! Marie LeClaire

This is a work of fiction. Any resemblance to actual events, locales, or persons living or dead, is purely coincidental.

ISBN: 9781703780024

Cover Art by https://selfpubbookcovers.com/Chthonika

"The most beautiful experience we can have is the mysterious. It is the fundamental emotion that stands at the cradle of true art and true science."
— Albert Einstein

Prologue

#995

It was 112 degrees and sunny, blindingly sunny. The dust, coupled with the dry desert air, was almost as lethal as the bombs. The shelling had gone on sporadically for three days now. In the silence in between, you could hear the wails of parents grieving for their children and the sobs of orphans wandering through the debris. Those that could, walked the streets calling out for anyone trapped in the rubble, listening intently for any reply.

Amid the wreckage, a young woman cradles her small son. He is bleeding and barely conscious. This is not Jihad, she thought. This is not God's will. This is slaughter and power-grabbing, the injury made all the worse because they claim the holy high ground as they aim the next rocket and let loose the next round of rifle fire.

She began singing the Janazah, the prayer for the dead, for her child, rocking with his body, back and forth to the rhythm of the chant.

In a cave deep in the Himalayas, a Buddhist monk stirs from his meditation. Opening his eyes, he gazes at the marks on the wall opposite him. Slowly rising from his cushion. He walks across the stone floor, picks up a piece of charcoal and uses it to cross a line through one of the hash marks. He bows his head, says a silent prayer, then slowly returns to his seat of straw and resumes his prayerful state, chanting first, then slipping back into meditation.

Chapter 1

#997

Nathan Morrison trudged along the rocky path through the Himalayan mountains in Nepal. The trail through the Annapurna Conservation Area was well above the tree line and fully exposed to the elements. Historically, it was a caravan route that connected the Kali Gandake River to the western interior. Today, the road stopped just past Manang, turning into a foot trail that almost faded completely into the rocky landscape, eventually connecting up to Kaisang.

With his hood sheltering him from the unremitting sun, he dragged Lucy, his less-than-cooperative pack mule, over the gravel path. He had dismissed the Sherpa yesterday in search of the true solitary experience. He planned to pick up another guide at the end of the pass, but for the next three days it was just he, Lucy, and the great Annapurna Wilderness.

Both Buddhists and Hindus considered the Himalayas to be sacred mountains. Judging from the view as he flew into

Katmandu, he could see why. They were expansive beyond anything he could have imagined. Snow-covered all year, the highest summits were rarely seen from the valley, disappearing into the clouds and inspiring a sense of mystery and majesty. Men had sought their peaks since the beginning of civilization. The tallest of all, Mt. Everest, was finally conquered in 1953 by Tenzig Norgay from Nepal, and Edmond Hillary from New Zealand.

Many came here on a spiritual journey. Nathan had no such grandiose goals. He'd given up on any great spiritual awakening after wasting $5,000 for a week-long workshop in Cabo, where overpaid scientists claimed that reality was just an illusion. True or not, it didn’t make much difference day to day. Life went right on ahead, with bills to pay and decisions to make. All he was hoping for now was that some solitude would clear his head. He needed to figure out what he was going to say to Kate.

The trail was safe enough. No rocky cliffs or wild animals. He’d come in November, despite it being the busy season, because that’s what fit into his jammed-up schedule. Usually, he traveled in the off season to avoid huge crowds. He chose this trail specifically because it wasn’t that popular. Not only would he avoid other hikers, but the chance of encountering any of the marauders that frequented the more touristy routes was as remote as the trail itself. He just needed to be alone, really alone. He needed to rid his mind of the chaos, stress and distractions of Chicago, to get clear about his future with Kate. Mostly, this trip was a stall tactic. She had laid down the ultimatum earlier this summer. Get in or get out of this relationship. In an effort to buy himself a few weeks, he concocted this life changing journey through sacred mountains to help him get his priorities straight. He’d seen the trip on a travel brochure in his dentist's office and it seemed as good an excuse as any and, who knows, it might work. So far, though, there had been no great insights.

After only a few hours without his guide, he was already feeling the discomfort of being alone with himself. Automatically, he reached for his cell phone in its usual place, on his side, attached to his belt. It wasn't there. He knew that. The reflex was purely habit. Whenever he felt disconnected or indecisive, all he had to do was log on and see what other people thought. It steadied him, gave him focus, clarified things.

Solitary life wasn't all it was cracked up to be. Nonetheless, he had three more days until he reached the next village so he resigned himself to make the best of it and focused his attention on the journey. That would be the Buddhist way, after all, focusing on the present moment.

It was late in the day and he was looking for a good spot to shelter for the night, somewhere out of the wind, somewhere level, maybe with a little cover in case afternoon rain clouds crept over the ridge. A small alcove in the massive walls of sandstone perhaps. It had worked for him the previous night.

The trail was visible for several miles as it wove its way through the barren mountainside. Beyond a couple of switchbacks, he could see the shadow of what appeared to be a small cave. Although it looked reasonably close, he knew from experience it would take at least two hours to get there, just in time for dinner. After conferring briefly with Lucy and meeting no resistance, he pressed on.

The sun was closing in on the horizon as he approached the alcove. The late afternoon stillness was comforting and he was looking forward to making camp. As he neared the entrance, he noticed a hint of fragrance in the air. It was a familiar smell. He recognized it from the various villages and temples he had been visiting along the route. It was Nag Champa, the incense of choice for most Buddhist practices. It had a distinct aroma. He looked around, curious about its source since he was miles from nowhere. The closer he got to the cave, the stronger the smell. He was beginning to wonder if his campsite was already occupied. It wouldn't be completely unheard of for some monk to be squirreled away up here, meditating, seeking enlightenment, but knowing how far they were from any village, it seemed unlikely. He cautiously approached the opening, leaving Lucy tethered just outside the entrance.

The scent was definitely coming from the cave. He poked his head in. As his eyes adjusted to the reduced light, he saw a typical cave with stone walls and dirt floor. No sign of habitation by man or beast. After stepping inside, scrapings on the back wall and ceiling became visible, indicating it had been expanded to sleep two or three travelers comfortably, with the ceiling raised to allow standing full-height for most people. A fire ring near the entrance indicated past use but there were no other signs of recent occupancy. Then he spotted a small portal in the rear wall that seemed to go further into the mountain. Walking toward the back, he picked up a slight humming sound. As he ventured further, it became a very distinct O-O-O-O-O-O-M-M-M-M-M-M. He recognized it immediately. It was an ancient Buddhist chant that, according to Eastern philosophy, aligned with the primordial sound of the universe. The sound just before the big bang. The sound before sound. He wasn't sure how much he bought into any of the eastern thought. At the moment he wasn't sure about anything except that so far, it had all seemed like a load of crap. Religion "is the opium of the people," Marx had claimed. He could believe that. Nonetheless, he had to admit that the steady hum of the chant was soothing and the possibility of human contact was appealing, even if it meant interrupting a holy man.

A faint light in the back drew him further into the cave. He followed the glimmer around a bend to discover a small chamber lit by a candle perched on a small stone ledge. Here he found the source of the chanting. In the dark red robes of the local temples, a monk sat perfectly still, chanting OM softly with each breath. Surely the monk had heard him. He wasn't exactly stealthy, tripping over boulders and crunching on the gravelly path, and yet the monk seemed undisturbed.

Nathan took the opportunity to look around the inner sanctum. It was about the same size as the outer room with similar scarring on the walls. On the dirt floor below the candle, was a small cache of dried food, a jug of water and a few blankets. To the right, the monk sat on some sort of a cushion, back to the wall and legs folded up like a pretzel. Opposite him, the left wall was entirely covered with hash marks as if the monk was keeping count of something. His gaze turned back to the man seated on the floor. He was old, very old. As Nathan considered this, the monk's eyes opened, startling him. They stared at each other for a long moment. Awkwardly, Nathan cleared his throat.

"Um, excuse me," he stammered, not sure if the monk even understood English. "I'm sorry to bother you."

The monk continued to look at him.

Thinking he didn't understand, Nathan went on, adding exaggerated hand gestures. "I'm s-o-r-r-y," he dragged out the words, waving hands of apology as he started to back out of the inner chamber.

"No problem," the monk replied in clear English. "Please stay."

"Oh," Nathan replied, aborting his retreat, "Yeah, sure."

After a moment the monk asked, "Why are you here?"

"Well, I was looking for a place to spend the night but-,"

"Why are you here in Nepal," the monk interrupted.

"Well, ah, not a simple question, really, but the short answer is that I'm hiking to Kaisang."

"Not where are you going. Why are you here?"

"I'm running away from my life."

"Not where have you come from," the monk replied patiently.

Frustrated, Nathan searched for the answer. "I'm confused, directionless, burnt out. I need clarity."

The monk nodded his acceptance. "You will find it here," he replied.

Nathan let out a noise that was almost a scoff. "That would be nice."

"You doubt me." The monk nodded his head. "Therein lies the problem. You doubt everything. Even your own judgment."

"No disrespect, sir, but it's complicated."

"It is not complicated. You make it so to avoid doing what you know is right."

Nathan considered this. It felt comfortingly true. He'd tried to dodge things but if he got honest with himself, he had known all along. He knew it when he got on the plane to find himself. He knew it standing in his boss's office the day the promotion was offered. He knew it when Kate laid out the ultimatum – marriage and family or move on. He knew the answers, he just didn't like them. This quest was more about looking for answers he liked.

Nathan looked down. “Maybe true,” he conceded.

“Stay. We have much to discuss, Nathan Morrison.”

A tiny ripple of fear ran through Nathan's body. He tried desperately to remember if he'd introduced himself when he entered the cave. He didn't think so, but the alternative was that he was expected. No, he must have told the monk his name. He just didn't recall it. Awkward self-doubt started to bubble through his external bravado. “But I've disturbed your peace,” he almost stammered, “I can find another spot.” He was back-peddling now.

“You can stay in the outer alcove. Settle yourself and attend to your animal,” the monk directed him. “Then return.”

Not seeing any graceful way out, he acquiesced. “Sure. Thank you.” He bowed awkwardly as he left.

Chapter 2

#997

When he emerged from the cave, the sun was low in the sky. Even if he wanted to, there wasn't much daylight left to find another camp site. He considered making a run for it. Whatever this was, he wasn't sure he wanted to get sucked in. Or was he already? And what was he doing here? This old monk had to be at least a little crazy to be sitting alone in the middle of a mountain a hundred miles from nowhere. Again, he consulted Lucy.

"Well, girl. What do you think?"

As if in direct response, Lucy placed her butt solidly on the ground, then tucked her front legs beneath her as she lowered herself to rest on the dusty trail.

"Are you sure?" he asked, hoping for a different outcome.

Lucy stayed put, turning her head away from him and looking out over the valley below.

"Thanks a lot," he mumbled as he started to untie her load. He secured Lucy at the entrance to the cave, attending to her food and water, then settled himself just inside, laying out his bedroll and organizing his supplies. Then return the monk had instructed. He wasn't sure he wanted to. He considered pretending to sleep and then sneaking out first thing in the morning. It felt a bit cowardly, even juvenile. Come on, he was better than that. He'd just been offered a promotion at his advertising firm making him the youngest manager ever promoted to director. What the hell was he afraid of?

In the corporate world he was known as a go-getter. He had a can-do and will-do attitude. He was all business, resulting in the all-work-no-play lifestyle that got rewarded with money and prestige. Kate had come along four years ago offering him legitimacy in a world where perceived monogamy was valued and a long-term relationship showed stability. At first, she fit into his picture more as an accessory than a staple. Now, however, with the threat of abandonment on the horizon, he was starting to appreciate how much he loved her. But was it enough for a lifetime? She wanted a long-term commitment. He was on thin ice and he knew it. Do or die. This trip to Nepal was partly just to placate her, proving that he was working on it. But he wasn't even sure what it was. And now, he was being offered the opportunity to take counsel with what millions of people considered a holy man and his response was to sneak away before daylight. Really? Who better to consult with – if you believed in that sort of thing? He was tired of the spiritual double-speak. Still, logic told him to hear the man out.

The sun was kissing the horizon good night when he headed to the back chamber. He tip-toed into the monk's space, secretly hoping he wouldn't be noticed. No such luck.

"Sit." The monk motioned toward the pile of folded

blankets on the floor.

"Thank you," Nathan replied as he made his way to the ground. His slender frame suggested an athleticism that had escaped him. Not being particularly flexible or graceful, his journey to the floor ended with a plop and a wince. Once seated, he looked around the cave again. It looked as if it had been used for many years. Soot from candles streaked up the walls and onto the roof. Straw mats on the floor showed signs of wear. His attention went again to the hash marks on the wall. He wondered if the monk was marking time. If so, it was a lot of days. Hundreds certainly.

"You think I mark time," the monk offered, as if knowing his thoughts. "You are incorrect."

Nathan, shaken a little by the comment, asked, "Then what do you count?"

"I count the Buddhas."

Nathan looked at the wall, then back at the monk. "I thought there were only four."

"As do most people. Their limited thinking discounts many."

Nathan looked back to the hundreds of lines on the wall. "How do you count them."

"A Buddha is a special being born with the ability to reach enlightenment. Not all do so. Some do not survive childhood. Others are enlightened but not recognized as such. Mother Theresa for example."

"I see."

The monk sat silently while Nathan contemplated this. "And Gandhi, maybe?"

"Yes. He is another."

"Why do you count them?"

"Are you familiar with the Buddhist teaching of 1000

Buddhas?"

"Yes, but only casually. That humanity will enter a new age after the 1000th Buddha is born." Nathan had learned a lot about Buddhism in recent days. It's hard not to, when you're walking through the Himalayas with a Sherpa. The story didn't get much attention, though, seeing that the most recently recognized Buddha, Siddhartha Gautama, was number four and born 2,500 years ago.

"True. But there is more to the legend. According to scripture, at least half must reach enlightenment, 500 or more. It is the tipping point so to speak, the critical mass as some current thinkers call it. And at least one must be alive and enlightened to lead us into the new age. My task is to count them."

"And what count are we at?" Nathan asked.

"999," the monk responded.

Nathan let out a gasp. "Are you saying that 999 Buddhas have been born? 995 since Gautama?

"Not technically," replied the monk. "Gautama was not number four. He was number eight. There were four born prior to him that died young."

Nathan looked at the wall again, following the rows of hash marks all the way to the end. The last four were uncrossed.

The monk continued, "There must be one more enlightened Buddha for humanity to evolve. Of the last five, four are currently alive, represented by the marks without a cross hash, and one is yet to be born. One of these five must reach enlightenment."

"How hard can that be?" Nathan asked.

"In today's world, it is very difficult."

Nathan looked at the wall that was full of crossed off

lives, then again at the last four.

"What happens if none get enlightened?"

"Humanity will spiral downward into generations of dark, painful times until every person is dead and humanity is extinct, leaving the earth to restore balance without mankind."

"Why isn't anyone out there protecting these Buddhas and babies?" Nathan demanded.

"It was decided from the beginning that the proper course was to allow each Buddha to experience their lifetime in whatever way unfolds for them and in the way of their choosing."

"Well, how's that working for you?" His tone had a hint of sarcasm.

The monk ignored the attitude. "The decision has recently changed and the plan is to protect each of the living Buddhas as best we can."

"Oh. Well, good then. I'm glad to hear it." Against his better judgement, he was getting drawn into the story. "Where are these Buddhas?"

"I don't know, exactly."

"What do you mean I don't know?"

"I am only aware of their birth and death. The vertical mark represents their birth. The cross-mark, their death."

"Well, that doesn't feel like a very efficient way to save the world from catastrophic darkness." Nathan's attitude was returning.

"Nonetheless, it is what we have."

"Well, someone knows though, right?"

"That is somewhat true. Others have various pieces of information."

"What do you mean?" Nathan wondered how much worse this was going to get. "You must know where they are, at least. You just said you decided to help them."

"Yes. That decision began the process for selecting individuals most appropriate to the task. The choice requires patience, the selection is of the highest importance."

"How long is that going to take?"

"It has recently been completed."

"I'll be heading back to the States in a few days. Let me know if I can help." It was a half-hearted offer of politeness.

"Indeed," replied the monk.

There was a pause. Nathan waited for the next comment. There was none. Then, before Nathan could fill the silence, the monk spoke again.

"You can stay as long as you like. I must go back into meditation for a few hours. We will talk tomorrow." With that, the monk closed his eyes and resumed his chanting.

Chapter 3

#997

Nathan returned to the inner chamber first thing in the morning to pay his respects and be on his way when the conversation took an alarming turn.

"Me! Are you joking?" Nathan strained to see the monk in the dim candle light.

The monk remained silent.

"Surely you have no idea who I am. I'm nobody. I'm a pebble in a ..." he struggled for an analogy. "I don't know, in a truck full of rocks. I'm nothing special."

The monk's continued silence added a level of urgency to Nathan's self-deprecation. "I'm certainly not a Buddha-hunting save-the-world kind of guy! I wouldn't even know how to start. The US is really big, you know."

"We know where he is."

"I thought you said you only know when they are born

and die?"

"That is all I know. We have others who search on the ground, so to speak."

"Great. Then just go get him."

"It is not possible in America today to walk into someone's home, claim their child is the next enlightened one, and take them to be raised in a monastery."

"Okay, maybe not. But surely there is another solution."

"There is. You."

"What do I know about being enlightened? About Buddhism? About any of it?"

"You do not need to know these things. We know these things. You need to know how to find someone and keep them safe in inner city America."

Nathan thought about this for a moment. It was certainly true that it would be nearly impossible for this man, or anyone like him, to navigate urban America without drawing a certain amount of attention. "Still, I'm not so sure I'm your man."

"We are sure."

"Who is this we you keep talking about?"

"Centuries ago, when it became apparent that Buddhas were dying at an alarming rate, the Dali Lama formed a secret order to hold the knowledge required to train the next Buddha. These individuals were stationed around the world. In the event that a Buddha was identified, they would be ready to act. That changed three years ago with the death of number nine hundred ninety-three."

"I'm still not clear who the we is."

"Trust that we are doing what we can, considering our limitations."

"That isn't an answer."

"That is my only answer."

Frustrated with where this was going, Nathan changed tacks. "Okay. So where is this person?"

"Chicago, Illinois."

The words hit him in the chest. Suddenly, Nathan saw the point of this whole conversation. He was scurrying around in his brain, looking for a way out. "Can you narrow that down?" His voice was louder than he expected.

"He is a male child, age thirteen."

"Seriously? Do you know how many thirteen-year-old boys there are in Chicago?" He was almost shouting.

"No. But we are sure you do."

Nathan stopped short. He couldn't argue there. Although he didn't know off the top of his head, it would be easy to find out, especially in his role as market developer. Maybe there was some method to the monk's madness.

"Okay, so let's say I do know. That's still a lot of boys. I can't just go ask each one 'Hey, are you the next Buddha?'"

The monk reached into a bowl beside him and retrieved a small pendant that he held up for Nathan to see. It was brass with a silver inlay of a seated Buddha on one side and what appeared to be a Sanskrit symbol on the other.

"This will help you identify him." He reached across the cave to Nathan.

Nathan held up his hands in protest. "I keep telling you, I'm not your guy."

"You are the only one."

"I'm not."

"You are."

Nathan looked at the medallion, then back at the old monk. Suddenly, he saw the monk differently. Canyons of age wrinkled his face and neck. Shadows under his eyes the flagship of sleep interrupted by worry. Ashen skin a likely indication of failing health. He realized he was looking at an old man carrying a great burden and it sobered him. He knew that by accepting the token, he was also accepting the task of safeguarding this young boy, whoever he was. He had to admit, the monk's story had rekindled some of the old mysticism he used to believe in. And it was plausible that he could identify such a boy if he existed. Still, he hesitated. Then, looking the monk directly in the eye, he slowly reached out across the cave. Both men paused for an almost imperceptible moment, exchanging the slightest of nods, a nonverbal agreement, before the medallion changed hands.

Nathan held it in his palm. It was small, about the size of a quarter, and otherwise unremarkable. It might be something bought from a street vendor at one of the local bazaars.

"What is it?" he asked.

"A talisman."

"Shouldn't it be bigger or grander or shinier or something."

The monk smiled, relieving the intensity of the moment. "Contrary to popular American opinion, size does not matter."

Nathan resisted the urge to defend himself. He had to agree that the Bigger is Better attitude had pretty much taken over American culture. With a nod and a smile, he asked, "How does it work?"

"It will react when you are within a certain radius of the child. The reaction will get stronger the closer you get."

"What kind of a reaction?"

"I do not know."

"Great." Nathan shook his head. He was starting to take this task seriously, as impossible as it sounded. "What if I fail?"

"Three more are currently alive and there is still one more

child yet to be born. They are the last hope for humanity to evolve."

"Okay. No pressure there," he replied, using humor to shake off the foreboding.

"Do not take this task lightly," cautioned the monk. "There is very little room for error."

Staring at the hundreds of charcoal hash marks, Nathan wondered what he was up against. "What happened to all those Buddhas?"

"They met their fates in various ways," offered the monk. "Some of natural causes, some in battle. One was buried alive in Pompei when Mount Vesuvius erupted in the first century. Twelve were executed as witches. Three died in the Black Plague. One in the concentration camps of World War II. Shall I go on?"

"No. I get the picture. Still, that's almost a thousand Buddha's in two thousand years. On average, one every two years." Nathan was thinking out loud.

"The further away from the last enlightened Buddha, the more frequently these special beings are born. When one reaches such a state, the birth rate slows again. But the world is becoming less stable and time is running out."

Nathan looked at the wall. The last four marks were free of a cross hash.

"Who decides when and where one is born?"

"By your understanding, God."

"Why doesn't God just make this transformation happen, regardless of the Buddha count?"

"God will not do for man what man will not do for himself. If we, as a species cannot accomplish this one seemingly simple task, we are not worthy of transformation and will thus die out."

"Not looking good for humans. What about the others? One is in Chicago under my watch. Where are the others?"

"They are likewise being guarded as best we can."

"By who?" Nathan was curious

"It does not matter. You have your task. Others have theirs."

Chapter 4

#997

Two days later, Nathan came down from the mountains a changed man. Whether the feeling was more lighthearted or burdened, he wasn't sure. But he knew he was different. He had finally found a depth to himself that he hadn't felt since his parents died. The world seemed three-dimensional again. It was the only way he could describe it. He looked ahead along the trail as it curved left and downward. The village had come into view as he rounded the last bend twenty minutes ago. Apparently, they'd spotted him as well. Now, he saw a tiny figure on the outskirts waving him in. He knew they would be waiting for him.

Originally, Nathan's plan was to hire another guide for the last leg of the hike. Now, he wasn't sure he wanted to be away for another week. He'd already spent an extra day at the cave, meaning he'd have to push hard to make up the time. It wasn't that he couldn't, but his talk with the monk changed things and he was feeling an urgency to get home. Their conversations played over and over in his mind during his decent from the mountains. At first, he'd wondered if he'd imagined it all. He had definitely spent a full day talking to a monk in a cave, hadn't he? Yes, he decided. That part was true. But the rest of it? The last Buddha? The end of times? Really? If it was a hoax, it was quite an elaborate one, and he didn't see any point in it.

Their conversations had been about much more than the young Buddha living in Chicago. Nathan had taken full advantage of the opportunity and asked all the questions he ever wanted to ask, about God, fate, suffering, even the meaning of life. He wasn't sure he understood all the answers, but it had given him a clarity that had been elusive in any of the workshops and traditions he'd studied. Then, as usual, doubt crept in. It was just like the monk said in their first encounter. He doubted what he knew to be true. The one thing that had become clear was his love and devotion to Kate. He would make the commitment she was asking for if she was still interested. What if she wasn't?

“Namaste!” he heard the man shout as he got closer to town. He waved back in acknowledgement.

“Namaste. Namaste,” the man greeted him as he entered the village amidst a flurry of activity.

“Namaste,” Nathan returned the greeting with a bow.

The man walked beside him, taking Lucy’s reins. They didn't get many hikers on this remote trail and people gathered to exchange news or sell provisions or trinkets. Nathan had agreed to carry a small mail satchel over the mountain, much like the pony express but slower and no pony.

In most villages, there was usually at least one person who spoke a minimal amount of English. Despite a thick accent, this man did better than most. “We have been waiting for you.”

“Really? How did you know I was coming?” Nathan

asked, wondering if there was some mystical grapevine.

"Brother, call me from Tilicho." The man held up a cell phone.

"What!" Nathan reached for his absent phone. "You have service?"

"Tuesday, Thursday only," the man replied. "Come," he commanded, as he led them toward the stables.

Usually, hikers traded out their pack animals from village to village, giving them a well-deserved rest. At the end of the season, a truck redistributed them back to their rightful homes for the winter.

"I've had a change of plans. I won't be continuing on. What is the best way back to Kathmandu from here?"

"Supply truck is waiting for you. Take you to city."

"How did you know that I would need a ride?"

"Monk told us."

"He has a cell phone?" Nathan asked incredulously.

"No be silly. No reception up there. He send us message three week ago."

"How did he know?" Nathan asked, confused.

"I not know. He just know. He tell us." The man shrugged his shoulders as if it was nothing out of the ordinary.

"Okay, never mind that." Nathan gave up trying to understand, for now, and focused on the supply truck. "When does the truck leave?"

"When you ready. Truck take you to Tatopani. Bus take you to Kathmandu. You clean up at hostel." The man indicated a small building on the far side of the plaza.

"Thank you," Nathan nodded to the man then turned to Lucy. "Thank you, old girl," he said as he untied his bundles. "You've been a real sport." Not being one for long goodbyes, he patted her briefly on the back before heading to an eagerly anticipated shower.

Chapter 5

#997

Kate was visiting her sister Mindy in Seattle while Nathan was off finding himself in Nepal. She also needed time away to think about her future. She and Mindy had been best friends all their lives and Kate didn't make a major decision without her. Their personalities balanced each other out nicely. Her sister could count on her for logic and a clear ethical compass, while she appreciated Mindy's attention to the feelings of others.

This week's meeting of the minds was taking place on a small island in Puget Sound that catered to summer visitors. Rentals were cheap in the off season and they took advantage of a discounted hotel room on the water. Closed up cottages and ice cream stands dotted the main roads. Once busy piers that offered whale watching tours and island-hopping excursions were mostly quiet, except for the dwindling weekend crowd. A small fishing industry kept the locals busy through the winter months, along with the seemingly requisite artist colony. Kate was going home with two small paintings and a hand-blown glass vase. Mindy, whose go-to splurge was jewelry, was sporting a new pendant and earrings carved from abalone shell.

It was an unusually warm morning and breakfast was on the deck of a small cafe overlooking the water, with the hazy Seattle skyline in the distance.

"Have you made the list?" Mindy asked. She was referring to the pros and cons list, her sister's standard starting point for decision-making of all kinds.

"I tried, Mindy. Really. But there are just too many variables, so, I had to presuppose some facts for each scenario." Her logical streak infuriated some people, but Mindy knew her better. Kate's emotional side was deeper than most people's, and when she felt things, it was always very intensely. So, she guarded her heart with reason.

"Okay. Let's hear them."

Kate spread two sheets of paper out on the table. "Supposition one is that Nate steps up to the plate and makes a commitment, like a mature adult."

Mindy smiled at the editorial.

Kate offered her own grin before continuing. "In that case there are these two possible scenarios with their accompanying pros and cons." She slid the first sheet forward.

"Okay. What else?"

"Supposition two is that he runs away like an adolescent boy before prom," she said, sliding the second sheet forward.

Mindy let out an audible chuckle. "Okay," she nodded. A gentle breeze threatened to sweep the pages into the Sound. Mindy quickly secured them with the salt and pepper shakers.

Kate went on, "In both cases, I allowed for keeping the baby or not keeping the baby. I figure if Nate does make the commitment, he might not be up for instant family."

"But Kate," Mindy protested, "you know you want kids. You've always wanted kids."

"I know. But it's an option. I'm not saying it's a good one, or my first choice, but I have to consider it."

"You really should tell Nathan about the baby, Kate. It's not fair to ask him to decide this without all the information." Mindy felt like Kate's logic was flawed on this point.

"He knows what I need from him and he knows it's an all-or-nothing deal at this point."

"He doesn't understand what's at stake," Mindy insisted. She loved Nathan and thought he was the perfect match for Kate. Her sister knew it, too, even if Nathan didn't.

"We've been through this, Mindy. I want Nathan to be in on principle not obligation."

"You're using this as some sort of test to see if he passes. It's not fair."

"My pregnancy is irrelevant. If Nathan is not ready to settle down, then the baby is just a trap." Kate was keeping a firm hold on her position.

"You're selling him short."

"I am not."

Mindy was lobbying hard now on Nathan's behalf. "Babies change things. When men find out they're going to be a father, it changes them. Just like it changes us. It's already changed you and you're not even sure you're having it."

Kate knew Mindy was right. Crazy, random mood swings had already made their way into her life at just six weeks. All logic was now tainted with emotional undertones. And things that were unimportant yesterday now required thoughtful decisions, like what to have for breakfast, and should she pass on parasailing this afternoon. The hormonal shift was undeniable, intrusive and more than a little annoying. “Can we move on to the lists, please?” she said, placing her palms flat on each sheet.

“For now,” Mindy yielded. She took a moment to review the lists, noting the color-coding and emojis her sister was known for.

“This is the desired outcome,” Kate said, indicating a list topped by two large happy faces with a smaller one in between surrounded by a rainbow of colors. “Nathan steps up, we have the baby and live happily ever after.” Then she moved to indicate another list topped by a frowny face colored gray. “This is the least desirable scenario. Nathan craps out for the last time. We split up. I get an abortion.”

Mindy winced slightly at the outcome.

“I know,” Kate reassured her. “I'm just saying, it's a possible scenario. I'm not sure I can handle having a baby on my own at this moment.”

“Right,” Mindy conceded. “But you can move out here and I can help.”

“Yes. I know. That's this option.” Kate indicated a third list topped by one large happy face and one smaller one highlighted in green. “But it has its own assumptions and the big one is that I get a job out here. Or I possibly stay in Chicago and hope Nate at least helps out, maybe changes his mind.”

“You could have a job here in a week. You know that.”

“No, I don't. I've been looking, just for sake of conversation, and you're right. There are a few possibilities but nothing is certain.” Kate sighed. “I need you to stay focused, Mindy, so please stop interrupting.”

“Okay. Sorry.”

“And, last but not least, is this.” The list was topped with two large faces with straight lines where the smiles should be. "It's the marry Nathan and have an abortion list."

Again, Mindy winced. Neither of the women were opposed to the option on principle, but they both knew that Kate wanted a family.

"This one has the most unknowns, the most what-ifs," Kate continued. "It has to come with the assurance of having a baby at a more opportune time. This one's running a close fourth. It's third only because of the variables."

"So," Mindy asked, "Nate has the next move?"

"Yes, he does." They both knew this whole exercise was more to prepare her emotionally for any outcome rather than actually making a decision. At the moment at least, the call was Nathan's.

"Please let me know as soon as you do. Honestly Kate, I think I'm more of a wreck than you are."

It was probably true. Kate was a little concerned that she wasn't more emotional about it, but she had been through this before with Nathan, many times. Now, it seemed tedious. Was it already too late for them? Had she written him off already? It was a variable she hadn't considered - until just now.

Chapter 6

#997

November in Chicago wasn't all that cold, but, as anyone will tell you, it's the wind, relentless and cutting, that can wear a person *down*. Comfortably tucked into his sixth-floor condo, it was easy for Nathan to doubt his experience in the mountains of Nepal. The unending decisions of ordinary life eclipsed the surreal encounter in the cave. Even still, nothing seemed the same. His old life now seemed colorless, without depth. Was it like that before and he hadn't noticed?

Even the city that he loved seemed different, he mused, as he looked out over downtown from his living room window. On the up side, it was the home of Wrigley Field and the Cubs. The Sears Tower held the title of tallest building in the world for twenty-three years, built by the world's largest retail company of the day, Sears and Roebuck. The city hosted two World's Fair Expositions, and brags some of the finest jazz music in the world. Nat King Cole and Benny Goodman are just a few of the greats that have called the city home.

Its recent claim to fame, as the most violent city in America, seemed in stark contrast to its glory days. But that's not entirely true. Chicago had always had its darker side. In 1896, J. J. Holms, the country's first known serial killer, was hanged after a suspected 200 murders. In 1929, Al Capone ordered the Valentine's Day Massacre, killing seven men execution style. John Dillinger was gunned down in the street by police in 1934. The city was dynamic, an angel today, the devil tomorrow. And now, somewhere in its midst, walked a thirteen-year-old Buddha.

He turned from the window to scan his apartment. Even this looked different. Kate's presence was everywhere. Photos here, little decorative touches there. Things he never would have bothered with.

She had used the time he was away to visit her sister in Seattle. Nathan knew it was partly to figure out her next step. If he wasn't ready for a family, then she needed to look for someone who was. He understood that. Until now, he had been reluctant to make the commitment. What if I'm wrong, what if we can't make it work, what if I'm a bad father, what if, what if, what if. The unknowns plagued him whenever he considered the life-long commitment she was looking for. He thought maybe he was caught up in the FOMO (Fear Of Missing Out) that plagued millennials? What if he met someone better? What if he got a great job offer far away? What if he wanted to quit the corporate world and become a surfing coach in Hawaii? Now he knew his fear wasn't any of these things. It had become clear to him in Nepal. The real fear was What if she dies on me like my parents did?

He was twenty-four. It was just a few months before he met Kate. It was still hard to believe. The knock on the door came just before midnight. It had woken him up. Two police officers stood in the breezeway of his apartment. There'd been an accident and could he come down and identify Sherman and Louise Morrison. There are some words you never want to hear he thought. From that moment forward, he'd been going through the motions. Until now.

His conversations with the monk had brought him out of his indifference. The world was three dimensional again, and along with it came all the sorrow and loss of that night that had been packed away with the household things. But along with it came a great love for Kate that he'd been holding at bay. As the monk had said, he knew what the answer was.

She had threatened leaving him more than once over the past four years. Each time he took a step closer. Now that he was ready, armed with a vision toward the future, he was a little panicky. Hopefully, Kate was still interested. He started to worry that he'd blown it, stalled for too long. Waiting for Kate's return, self-doubt inched its way in.

He would commit to the new job as well. Not out of loyalty or love of the company but because now it was a means to an end. The position, Second Assistant to the Vice Director of Market Development (who made this shit up?) would allow him freedom to move around the city, exploring new market potential. He'll have access to all levels of society from wealthy entrepreneurs to neighborhood non-profits. What better way to search for #997, if it was all true? He reached for the medallion hanging around his neck, looking for a sign, some reassurance. Holding it in his hand, it appeared little more than a tourist trinket. Maybe it was.

The airport was a madhouse as usual. He waited just outside the security area carrying a large bouquet of flowers. Kate's flight had landed fifteen minutes ago but it seemed like forever, waiting to spot her coming through the terminal. They had talked only briefly in the two days since he'd been back. She seemed a little distant on the phone and he was nervous. He needed her to be on board. He needed to tell her about his great adventure, about his new understanding of what's important. He was barely breathing when he saw her coming down the walkway. His heart pounded in his chest. She looked more beautiful than ever. He fought back tears as waves of emotion threatened to break the male code - thou shalt not cry.

She smiled when their eyes met. It was a smile he knew. It was her *I'm glad to see you* smile. He let out a breath and smiled back, reaching out for her at the first opportunity, sweeping her up for a long embrace.

"Well, that's a nice welcome."

"I missed you," he said as he kissed her on the cheek and handed her the bouquet.

"I missed you, too."

He grabbed her rolling carry-on and shopping bag, which weighed more than he expected.

She laughed at his expression. "A glass vase."

"Please tell me it's not a Chihuly." Unarguably the greatest glass artist that ever lived, Chihuly called the Seattle area home, with small hand-blown items for sale at his main studio and workshop, starting in the thousands of dollars.

"No, not that bad. But it wasn't cheap – and you'll love it."

He stacked the package onto the handle of the rolling bag and took her hand as they joined the tide of humanity heading for baggage claim.

"From the sounds of it, you've had quite an adventure," she commented.

"I have. Life changing. Really." He gave her hand a squeeze.

"I can't wait to hear about it."

"I want to hear about your adventure, too."

"Visiting my sister in Seattle isn't exactly an adventure," she laughed, "although there were some dicey moments getting to and from the airport. Really, I don't know how she does it."

There was the expected small talk while they watched the luggage carousel go around. The weather, the traffic, the state of the apartment.

"I've done all the laundry and gone grocery shopping. Wong's is holding a takeout order for dinner tonight. I thought it would be easiest to just go home and relax." Wong's Asian Fusion was one of their favorite spots for dining in or out.

"Okay, what did you do with Nathan?" she asked sternly.

He smiled. "I know, right. I'm telling you, it was quite a trip."

They arrived at the conveyor belt, which was already circling with a menagerie of luggage and packages. They watched as other people's belongings rolled by.

"Well, whatever happened, it all sounds fabulous. Visiting Mindy was great, but I think I need transition time," she sighed. "I'm glad we planned a few days off before we go back to work."

"Me, too. I'm still trying to catch up to the jet lag."

They both had high pressure jobs with young start-up companies trying to redefine the marketplace. He was an urban planner in market projections. She was a graphic artist in digital marketing and social media. Despite the new concept of a low stress, highly creative workplace of the dot-coms, they still worked long hours under deadlines with high expectations. But they were young and riding the wave. At the moment it seemed more like excitement than stress.

"I say tomorrow we don't even get dressed. Sit around, watch TV, and lots of sex."

"I can work with that." She smiled and inched in a little closer to him. "Oh, and there's my bag."

Nathan stepped up and retrieved the familiar green suitcase that had accompanied them on many occasions. He imagined it covered with stickers from all their travels, like the boxy leather suitcases of old. Today, the ragged edges from many conveyor belt journeys told the same story. It was a testament to the new young professional's thirst for adventure first, then a pet, then maybe children. Was the wear and tear a harbinger of changes on the horizon?

Chapter 7

#997

Kate was spreading the takeout boxes onto the kitchen table. The kitchen was small but manageable, with just enough room for a table in the center allowing them to use the intended dining space as more of an office. Nathan chattered nervously as he reached into the cupboard for dishes.

"So, what did you do in Seattle? You and your sister must have talked a lot. Completely contrary to my vacation, which was oddly silent. It's amazing what goes through your mind when you're not engaged with someone." Hearing his own Freudian Slip, he nervously overcorrected. "Ah, not engaged exactly but... well, you know what I mean."

Kate looked up from the table. "What's wrong with you?"

"What? I'm fine."

"You seem nervous."

"No. No. Not exactly. Well, I guess maybe, a little." He put the dishes down and wiped his now-sweating hands down the front of his jeans. "The truth is, I had an amazing experience in Nepal. Really. Like all those woo-woo stories that you hear about." He was calming down a bit.

Kate, on the other hand was now anxious. She knew this was the conversation and she was unclear which way it was going. "I'm happy for you," she tried to sound sincere.

"Yes. And part of this amazing experience, a vision, well, not a vision exactly, you know, not like psychic or something but well..."

"Nathan?" she interrupted.

"Yes?'

"Is there a point here?"

"Yes," he exhaled sharply in frustration. He ran his fingers through his hair, interlocking them behind his head and looking down. "I so suck at this. I'm screwing it all up," he said to the floor. "I can't even propose right," he grumbled. Then, realizing he had said that aloud, he looked up, surprised at himself. "Ah, shit!" He threw his hands up in the air. "What I'm trying to say, the point you asked for, is that I want to marry you but it's coming out all wrong! I know I'm not the most romantic guy in the world, but I thought I could at least do better than this? I've been rehearsing it for two days!"

"Nathan?' Kate interrupted again.

"Yes?"

She walked around the table and took his hands in hers. "Take a deep breath. Get out of your head and into your heart. Then tell me what you want to tell me."

Nathan looked into her eyes, struck again at how beautiful she looked. Radiant, really. Had he never noticed before? Taking a deep breath and squaring his shoulders, he went on, "I love you. You know that. I hope you know that. Even though I might not be so good about showing it, and about the long run, so to speak. I know you've been looking for that and I'm sorry that I haven't stepped up. I know it's been hurtful to you, kept you off balance, wondering what to do next. My time in Nepal was oddly – well, odd, and I can't wait to share it all with you." He took a moment to squeeze her hands and refocus his thoughts. "In any event, suffice it to say that I have a new clarity about things, lots of things, but what I want most in my life is for you to be my wife and my partner, to be able to give you everything you want in life, without exception." He paused, holding tightly now to her hands, and waited.

Kate held her excitement in check. She wasn't sure where to go with this sudden turn of events and she needed to know the extent of what he was offering. "And children?" She cut right to the chase. This had been a sticking point for them.

"As many as you like," Nathan replied without blinking.

She looked at him for signs of hesitation and found none. Still doubtful, she remained silent.

He brought her hands up to his lips and kissed them. Then, he looked again into her eyes. "Trust me when I tell you, things have changed. I have changed. I'm clear. There is nothing I want more in my life."

Kate's wall of logic dissolved into tears that she had been holding at bay, not wanting to give them any airplay until she was sure he was sure. "Yes," she declared through her tears.

He immediately wrapped his arms around her, kissing her with a passion he had never felt before.

"When can we start having children?" she whispered in between kisses.

"How about now?" he responded, pulling her even closer, pressing their bodies together.

"Good. Because I'm pregnant." It was out of her mouth before she could stop it, before she could think it through. She held her breath.

"What?" Nathan stepped back, held her at arm's length and looked into her eyes again. Of course. Why hadn't he seen it at once? The radiance she had taken on in his absence, the overwhelming love he was feeling for her at this moment. He wasn't the only one who had changed.

Recovering from the shock, he began to laugh. "Of course you are." He swept her into his arms and spun her around the kitchen, whooping and laughing and kissing her belly.

Kate laughed right along with him. "I'm really looking forward to hearing about your trip to Nepal," she kidded him.

"And I'll tell you about every bit of it. But not right now." He held her tightly as he danced her to toward the bedroom.

Chapter 8

#997

Nathan was settling into his new office when the Director of Marketing came by to welcome him.

"Good to have you on board, Nathan. I'm looking forward to a fresh pair of eyes with a vision for the future." His new boss, Adam Richards, reached out to shake his hand.

"I'm glad to have the opportunity," Nathan replied as he returned the handshake. "I've had some great ideas while I was away and there's one in particular that I want to start with." Nathan held the handshake a little longer than usually expected, preventing Adam from making a quick exit. "I'm thinking that a fair number of our clients are targeting the young professional population so, my idea is to research and connect to the next young professionals. Teenagers." He released Adam's hand when he knew he had his attention. "What do you think?"

Adam held up a hand in protest. "Whoa. Back it up, Nathan. You know the firm has always been clear on that. We do not market to children."

Nathan went on quickly, "Not marketing to them. Just listening to them, getting to know them. What are their ideas about the future? How do they see themselves? With a few strategic questions, we can be ahead of our market by ten years or more. Not defining today's marketing strategy, but one for the future, so when it gets here, we're ahead of the game."

Adam paused in his protest to consider the idea. "How are you thinking this will work?"

"We set up a community-based service or outreach, like a scholarship fund or sponsor sports teams or something, so we get our fingers into the next generation in a grass roots kind of way. Not a Gallup Poll and not analyzing current market trends, but by getting into the heads of the next gen. Growing with them." Nathan checked to make sure his new boss was with him. Adam hesitated, then gave him a nod to continue.

"Maybe we buy sports equipment for a few of the poorer schools. Sponsor fund raisers for children's issues. I have a hundred ideas. There'll be an initial outlay of cash, offset eventually by corporate and local sponsors. But if you keep to that idea about a vision for the future, it will pay itself back in spades."

"Hm. I like it. Write it up and have it on my desk ASAP." Adam turned and headed out the door without waiting for a response.

"Yes, sir. Consider it done," Nathan called after him.

Chapter 9

#998

Sarah Sullivan was at a decision point in her young life. What next? Stay or go or something else. Returning to Nebraska felt like step backward, like putting on clothes that were out of style and no longer fit. Remaining on Guam had its own drawbacks. Low pay and limited opportunities made the island feel confining. She needed space, lots of space. When she saw the pictures in the travel agency window, she knew what she had to do. A walk-about at the foot of the highest and most sacred mountain range in the world, the Himalayas. Surely, she could find clarity there. She was not disappointed.

Sarah's life changed forever the day she stumbled upon the cave in the mountains of Nepal. She realized now that it wasn't stumbling at all but divine intervention. It was exactly what she was looking for. Direction. Intention. Purpose. Charged with the task of keeping one infant alive seemed both simple enough, except for the circumstances. She felt seriously unqualified for the task of caring for the next Buddha, but the monk had assured her she would have the support she needed when she needed it. But how will she know what to do when, or even if she finds this child? She didn't even know the first thing about Buddhism.

"Your task is to find him and ensure his safety. Ours is to show him the way to enlightenment," the monk had instructed.

"I know Guam isn't that big, but it's still 200,000 people. That's a needle in any haystack," she protested.

"The special one is an infant boy, born just three weeks ago."

"Okay. So, a needle in half a haystack," she bemoaned.

"You will find him. We are sure."

"Well, I'm not."

"You will have this."

The monk had given her a nondescript medallion and instructed her to wear it always and against the skin or it's efficacy would diminish. Looking at it now as it lay on her chest, she realized it rested directly over her heart chakra. According to many Eastern religions, there are at least seven energy centers in the body, each corresponding to a specific area of life. The heart chakra was the most obvious one. Its energy was love and its area of influence was relationships. She thought about the baby. How was she going to stay close to him, assuming she could find him? She would need to develop a supportive relationship with him and his family if she was to complete her task. A goal that might take her entire life. Or a good portion of it anyway. What was she thinking when she agreed to this insanity? It all seemed so reasonable in a cave in Nepal. Back on the island, it bordered on ridiculous. It was her own fault really. She had gone to the Annapurna wilderness on a quest to find purpose in her life. She sure got one.

Getting to anywhere from Guam was an ordeal. That's why almost no one did it. It had taken her twenty-eight hours, three airports, and two airlines to get back home. She'd spent almost as much time traveling as she had hiking. To most Guamanians, she was a little strange that way, wanting to travel, see the world. To be honest, most people in Nebraska thought so too. She got more than one confused look when she left three years ago, just days after her college graduation. She had taken advantage of the Reach Out to America program, an opportunity to have student loans forgiven in exchange for working in underserved areas around the country. She had no idea that Guam was part of the United States, but when she saw it, she jumped at the chance. Now, three years later, her commitment was over and she was trying to decide what was next. When she confided in her closest friend on the island about her ambivalence, her friend was quick to advise with every saying ever printed on a plaque. Follow your passion. Look within. Be courageous. You already know the answer. Spirit will guide you. Timaria was always encouraging her to look for the spiritual in the mundane. But Timaria was happy here, surrounded by family and friends. Sarah still felt as disconnected as she had when she first arrived. Timaria had suggested a few weeks traveling.

"You should go to Nepal. That's where headquarters is for my Buddhist temple. I've always wanted to go there. But I probably won't."

The last comment summed up the island attitude completely. They loved the idea of an adventure but not the reality of it. When she saw the advertisement in the window, she took it as a sign.

She spent most of the trip home strategizing her next move. She currently worked as a social worker for a local non-profit. They had asked her to stay on as a part-time regular employee after the Reach Out contract was over. Even though it cut her hours in half, it paid almost the same as the stipend she was getting from the government which wasn't much. Fortunately, she hadn't given them a response, asking for time to think about it. It proved to be a good move. The job would be a good starting point for her new task, to find the Buddha. But how could she possibly identify and visit each newborn on the island? It's not like she could simply look up the birth records for that day and start making the rounds. Or could she?

"Well, Sarah, we are certainly happy to have you stay on." Rita Ortiz, the director of Building Futures, a privately funded social services agency, sat behind her large oak desk. For a man, it might have been a sign of power. For Rita, it was simply a gigantic work surface covered with papers and files. "But really, you can take a few more days if you like. There's no rush."

"Thank you, Rita, but I'm good to go, really. I'm excited to start as a regular employee."

"As long as you're sure?"

"Totally. And besides, while I was away, I had this amazing idea and I couldn't wait to run it by you." Sarah was sitting on her hands, trying to curtail her excitement.

"I appreciate your enthusiasm, but it can wait another day

until your paperwork is all in."

"Nope. I got it under my skin now and you know how I am. I want to run with it so I'm hoping that you think it's a great idea too."

"Okay, then." Rita relented with a smile. She put the papers she was holding onto the nearest pile and leaned back in her chair. "Go."

"I'm thinking that if we reach out to every young family, even if they don't need our services, then we have a connection from the very beginning. They might never need us but they might know someone who does or they might be a resource in the future, for volunteers or donations." She paused to check Rita's interest.

"I'm listening," Rita nodded.

"I start by visiting all the newborn families, bring a small gift of some kind, you know, something that all moms need, like a certificate for a hot meal delivered from a local restaurant, or a bag of diapers. We get these things donated by local merchants. Then we follow up regularly over time, as needed. If nothing else, just to remind them we're here." She paused to take a breath.

"This sounds like a huge project, Sarah. How do you propose we staff it and pay for it?" As director of a non-profit, Rita was always concerned with the bottom line.

"Well, I figure that the work can be distributed to existing departments, at least initially, like Fund Raising, Outreach, Volunteer Services, Mother's Helpers, and the like, so it might not mean a whole lot of extra work for one person. And then, as the program gets going, we can see what we need and how to fine tune it. The birth rate averages around twenty per day, but that's over the whole island. We can start here locally and see how it goes." By locally, she meant Dedado, the island's largest village, totaling roughly 45,000 people.

"And when do you plan on doing all this? You already have a very full part-time schedule."

"Yes. I know I have. But if you can give me just a few more hours, I'm sure I can get it off the ground in a matter of days."

Rita tilted her head and raised her eyebrows. "Really? Aren't you being overly optimistic?"

"Okay, maybe a week or two. Tops."

"Okay. If you write it up, with a time budget for other departments, I'll float it at the manger's meeting tomorrow."

"Yes!" Sarah pulled her hands out from under her legs and raised them in victory.

"Don't get all over this yet, Sarah," Rita cautioned. "The managers still have a say."

"I know they'll love it. I'll get that proposal to you by this afternoon." Sarah popped out of her chair. "Thank you. Thank you. Thank you," she called over her shoulder as she headed out of the office.

Chapter 10

#997

The temperature was dropping along with the sun and the orange rays cast long shadows over the streets of Chicago. It was a blessing of sorts for Devon Johnson. The encroaching darkness swallowed up the empty liquor bottles and used needles lurking in the alleys and doorways of his neighborhood. The evening chill made the temperature at home seem warm in comparison.

It was already dark when he unlocked the door to their low rent apartment just before 5 pm. The initial relief from the cold would be short-lived so he didn’t take his coat off. His mother always turned the heat down so they didn't run up a bill she couldn't afford. If he turned it on before she got home, there'd be hell to pay. Her arrival home didn't guarantee the heat went on and most nights he slept fully dressed, bundled up in an old quilt from the thrift store. His bed was a mattress on the floor.

School was his respite. It kept him fed and warm during the day. He stayed late whenever he could, going to every sports event and club possible even though he hated them all.

His misunderstood interest in school activities made him a favorite of the teachers. They were constantly telling him how good it would all look on his college application…as if he were going. Today's event, a JV basketball game, was painful to watch. He wasn't much of an athlete himself but he could tell suck when he saw it. He was glad he had homework to distract him.

He entered the chilly apartment and looked up at the clock. His mom would be home soon. He wasn't sure from where. She said she had a job, but was a little sketchy on the details. He knew not to ask. He headed toward the kitchen which was usually the warmest spot in the apartment. He figured it was because it shared a wall with the next unit. On unbearably cold days, he would turn on the oven for brief periods. If his mother noticed, she never said.

She saved the heat for when her boyfriend, TJ, came over. She treated him like he was something special, but Devon knew him for what he was. A bully and a drunk. He didn't blame TJ though. Those were the kind of guys his mother picked. Users and abusers. At thirteen, he'd already figured out the lay of the land as far as his mother was concerned. It wasn't complicated. Men first, Devon last.

He was pulling out the last of his homework when he heard footsteps on the stairs. Maybe she'd be bringing dinner with her. If not, he'd have to figure something else out. The door popped open and his mother, Nadine, rushed in, closing the door behind her. He heard her go directly to the thermostat and turned on the heat.

"Hey, sweetie baby. Where are you?" she called out.

Devon came around the corner from the kitchen. "Hey mom. TJ coming over?"

"Ya. How'd you know? Sometimes I think you're psychic

or something."

He shook his head. "Just a good guess."

"Hey. Maybe you can go over to Jamie's house and do homework or play or something."

This was his mother's code for I have no food for you. Will Jamie's mother feed you?

"Yeah, that'd be cool. I told him today I'd come over if I could." This was his code back for Yeah, I get it. TJ's bringing food, but not for me.

"That's nice. Well, have fun. Make sure you finish your homework." Code for Don't come back before ten.

"Yeah. Sure," was all he could say.

He knew he had a few minutes before TJ arrived. In the warmer months, he would get his things together and head out the door, but December was too cold to be hanging outside for very long and he was hoping to enjoy the heat for a few minutes before he had to leave. Just then there was a knock at the door and TJ let himself in. That was Devon's cue. He slid past TJ at the door on his way out.

"Hey. See you later, kid," TJ snarled at him as he past.

At least the house would be warmer tonight, he thought, as he wandered around the neighborhood, and maybe there'd be leftovers. In the meantime, he had nowhere to go. He was over at Jamie's last night and Byron's two day before that. He tried to rotate through the few friends he had, so as not to wear out his welcome. He wasn't sure how much other parents knew, but they were all polite about his usually unannounced arrival around dinner time. When he was short on a place to go, he looked for the older kids who ran around the streets. It wasn't the best company - they were usually running drugs - but they were nice to him and sometimes bought him a hamburger or a taco. Devon knew they were trying to coax him into the gang. He didn't care.

Chapter 11

#997

Nathan's proposal, to visit all eighteen middle schools in the city with scholarship programs, had been heartily endorsed by Adam. Now, he had to walk his talk. He was fingering the chain around his neck that held the medallion as he paced his office. His colleagues thought he was a little odd when he rearranged his office to clear a maximum stretch along the longest wall for this purpose. But pacing allowed him to focus. Now, he was thinking about a thirteen-year-old boy in a city of 2.7 million people. He stopped to gaze out the window at the busy street below. People hustled past, bundled against the winter wind that swept down the funnel created by the tall buildings on either side of the street. Cars constantly moved in all directions. Hundreds of people in just the area he could see from this fourth-floor view. What had seemed possible from a cave in the Himalayan mountains, now felt ridiculous. There were simply too many factors at play.

The whole plan hinged on the assumption that the boy

was enrolled in school somewhere and was in his appropriate grade. A series of intramural activities would bring most of the students together eventually. What if he was out sick the day Nathan visited? What if he was kept back and Nathan was looking in the entirely wrong place? What if he went through all the schools and didn't find him? These scenarios were just a distraction from the real question that plagued him. What if he failed the monk? What had started out as a challenge, even a matter of pride, had become much more compelling. He felt an urgency that, if he wasn't careful, would become an obsession, blotting out everything else. Kate had warned him about this.

"Your job isn't something to be used to further your personal goals. It's a bad idea." Kate was standing at the kitchen counter waving a large knife at him.

Nathan was pacing the kitchen-dining room transit. "Do you have a better one?"

"Yeah. My idea is that the old monk was out of his mind and he sucked you into his delusion." She turned back to chopping vegetables.

Kate's enthusiasm for the Buddha Mission, as they were calling it, ebbed and flowed with her mood swings. On good days, she was keeping track of his progress. On bad ones, she worried that his priorities were unclear. She couldn't argue that something profound had happened in Nepal, but her focus was different now. She was pregnant. That took priority over everything.

"Come on, Kate. We've talked about this. You could be right." Nathan threw his hands up as he paced. "Now that I'm back here in Chicago and back with you and planning a future," he flashed her a smile, "I'll admit, it does seem a little odd. But he was so compelling, so convincing. You weren't there. You don't know. I have to do this."

"Even if you find him, how are you going keep him safe? From what? And what does that even mean? Is this kid in some kind of trouble? Because that's the last thing we need right now."

"We don't know anything yet. Maybe he's a good kid from a good neighborhood and all we need to do keep an eye on him."

She turned with the knife in the air again. "You," she corrected him. "All you need to do is keep an eye on him."

"Okay. Okay." He raised his hands in surrender. "Stop waving that thing around."

She placed the knife on the counter and dumped the veggies into a pot of water.

"I get it. Just me. Fair enough," he conceded. He knew her interest would be piqued again as things moved forward. She was a problem-solver by nature. She'd already given him some great ideas for middle school activities.

"That being said," she continued, "I have been doing a little research."

"I see." Nathan tried not to grin. It didn't work.

"What?" she defended herself, struggling to suppress a smile of her own. "I'm not disinterested. Just cautious."

"Sure. Whacha got?" Nathan asked, still grinning.

Preoccupied with developing a reasonable program at work to flush the boy out, he had no clue what he would do after that.

"It appears," Kate went on, "that there are several branches of Buddhism, kind of like Christianity and Judaism. Each with its own slants on the teaching and its own focus of practice." She placed the pot on the stove and turned on the heat.

"Any of them supporting the one thousand Buddha teachings?" Nathan asked.

"It's hard to say right now, but I did find something interesting in Montana."

"Seriously?" Nathan stopped his pacing and looked up. "Montana?"

"I know, right? Believe it or not, there's a place called The Garden of a Thousand Buddhas. It's in the middle of nowhere, about twenty miles north of Missoula. From the pictures, it looks like a nice, well-kept garden, like it says, with one thousand statues of the Buddha."

"Wow! Really?"

"Yes. Really."

"You're amazing. Okay. Let's go." Nathan was jazzed by the news.

"Hold on a minute. You're forgetting that we both have jobs that we just took a vacation from."

"That was two months ago."

"Two months is not that long in corporate time."

"I suppose not," Nathan conceded.

"And, I might point out, it's December. And if you think life is miserable in Chicago, you won't like Montana at all."

"Oh, yeah." Nathan's mood was quickly deflating, "Another good point."

"However, I do have some time tomorrow that I could get on the phone and at least talk to them."

"You are the best." He came up behind her, pulling her close and cradling her belly which was beginning to show the existence of the baby growing inside. "You're going to be a great mom." He mumbled as he kissed her neck.

"Yeah, well, I'd like to be a great wife first." She

squirmed out of his arms. “So, Nathan Morrison, when are you going to make an honest woman out of me?” With the holidays upon them, discussion of a wedding seemed to be back-burnered and Kate was concerned that time would diminish Nathan’s resolve.

“Today, if you want, but your sister won’t like it much. And then there’s your cousin Linda in Maryland.”

“Sure. Blame my family. But if we wait much longer, I’ll be wearing a maternity wedding dress.”

“Okay. We’ll talk about it this weekend. I promise.”

They knew it would be a small event. Kate’s family consisted of her parents in New York, and her sister in Seattle. Nathan had an aunt in Sacramento, and an uncle in Idaho. A few close friends scattered around the country would fill out the guest list.

“We have to give people at least a little notice,” Kate persisted.

“I’m not sure anyone in my family will come, in any event.”

“I know. I’m sorry your parents aren’t here.”

“Yeah, well,” Nathan got quiet. He recalled the monk’s words. “Everything happens in its own time.” When Kate looked up at him from the stove, he realized he’d said it out loud. “The monk’s response when I asked him about it.”

Sirens on the street below Nathan’s office shook him out of his mental review of tasks. Things had moved quickly once they set a date, which was New Year’s Eve, on a charter boat on Lake Michigan. The guest list totaled eighteen. Surprisingly, his uncle and aunt, and their respective spouses, had accepted the invitation. Nathan assumed it was out of sympathy. Nonetheless, he was glad they were coming. It was he who had distanced himself over the years, not them. Part of his new view of the world included a healthy appreciation of family. He hoped he hadn't burned the bridge too badly. Their acceptance of the invitation was a good sign.

Chapter 12

#996

Akio stood on the sea wall, looking down into the water of Sekate Bay. The ocean off the coast of Okinawa, Japan, was known worldwide for its clarity, and he could easily see fifteen feet below the surface to the rocks and coral that formed the island's coastline. He studied the usual sea creatures as they swayed with the current. There were the spidery black starfish that clung loosely to the rocks, the crabs that seemed to jump in surprise with each wave, and the dozens of little sunfish that would soon become dinner for those further up the food chain. He had never imagined he could have such a peaceful life. When he played back the chain of events that got him here, it was almost unbelievable.

He had arrived from Tokyo six months earlier, coming on what he thought to be a fool's errand - to find a young girl born to Buddhahood and then ensure her safety. He was sure his search would fail. Nonetheless, he had made a commitment to the monk and he was obligated to see it through as best he could. His strategy had been to start at the north end of the island, where the sparse population was centered in small fishing ports and farming villages. If he got all the way to the southern end, where the population was much denser, the task would become nearly impossible. As it turned out, it wasn't as hard as he thought. He had created a story about finding a long-lost cousin, a twenty-three years old female. Family being very important to the culture, most people were happy to help. Being single and twenty-eight didn't hurt either. Every young single woman in each village came out to say hello. In almost no time, he found her here, in Sekate, a peaceful fishing port on the northeastern coast.

He remembered when they first met. He was struck by her beauty even before the medallion pointed him in her direction. In fact, he had thought at first that the sensation in his chest was his own heart pounding in response to such a beautiful woman. When the realization came that the monk's pendant was responsible for the electric charge running through his body, he both laughed and panicked. He never expected to actually find her. The monk's instructions had been clear. You must keep her safe at all costs. The task seemed easy enough in a village where crime was almost non-existent, save the occasional disorderly drunk.

Kasumi was a no-nonsense young woman, as mature for her age of twenty-three as he was immature for his age of twenty-eight. Her parents owned a small supply shop on the wharf that catered to the fishing boats. As their only child, she was obligated to stay and help with the business, but she didn't mind. Unlike most people her age that were running off to mainland Japan to find their fortunes, she loved it here.

At first, she dismissed Akio as some wild child, running away from trouble in Tokyo and concocting a story of a monk and a secret cave to worm his way into her good graces. He had to admit, in the past that might have been true, but his trip to Nepal had truly changed him. He was duty-bound and committed to complete the monk's request if it was in his power to do so. Kasumi's safety was his life now. He had done his best to explain things to her. He told her about the 1000th Buddha, the wall of hash marks, the end of times. Having been raised Buddhist, she at least had a basic understanding of what he was saying. Still, she was hard-pressed to believe herself the next enlightened being. He had to show her the medallion, let her feel its message, in order to sway her thinking.

Once Kasumi was on board, the next step was making a connection to the local temple. The island itself had been almost entirely rebuilt by the American occupation forces after the Battle of Okinawa left few structures intact, even in the smallest of villages. The Buddhist temple, however, had somehow survived the conflict with minimal damage. A modest brick and wood building in the pagoda style that hearkened back hundreds of years, it was a stark contrast to post-war simplicity. Most buildings sported a plain concrete block design easily shipped in from nearby allied bases and assembled quickly. The local people did a noteworthy job beautifying their boxy facades with brightly colored paint depicting imagined architectural detail. The down side was that the paint peeled quickly in the tropical environment and needed constant attention.

The temple housed one monk who served the community here in Sekate and the three surrounding villages. He had been skeptical of Akio's story, insisting that he was in no way prepared to instruct anyone at the level required by his request, no matter how much Akio pleaded. The monk tired of Akio’s constant pestering and contacted the home office for direction. Akio’s persistence paid off and a Master teacher arrived to oversee Kasumi's lessons.

Despite being on a monastic path, vows of austerity and celibacy were years away and he and Kasumi had grown close. She managed to dance back and forth across the line between religious devotion and secular interests. It seemed to be a happy medium that even the Master could live with. He knew from experience that initiates needed to understand completely the choice they would eventually make.

Akio was on his way to his apartment in town when the sirens went off. He'd heard them before. It was the tsunami warning system. They tested it monthly. But it was usually preceded by an announcement of the test. This time there was no explanation. It took a second to register why. This was not a test! There was a wave headed their way! Adrenaline shot through his system. He had to act fast. Where was Kasumi? He had left her a few minutes ago at the dock. He had to find her. Without hesitating, he turned and began running back the way he had come, towards the shore.

He ran with the slow motion of nightmares. Memories of their time together began flashing though his mind. He pushed against the crowds. Their yells sounded like long-drawn-out echoes. He looked to the Buddhist temple on his right as he ran past, wondering for an instant if the monks were out looking for her as well.

The medallion hanging from his neck was causing a shooting pain in his chest, reminding him of his mission. Still running as if through invisible molasses, he maintained a laser focus, scanning the faces running past him to higher ground. He spotted the cafe where they had eaten just a few minutes ago. She would have been headed back to her family's shop on the wharf, in the other direction, when the warning sounded. How far had she gotten? What route would she take? Would he miss her going the other way, making his headlong dash into peril futile? It didn't matter. His life was unimportant. He knew in his heart it was a lost cause, that he had failed both the monk and Kasumi. Why hadn't he considered the danger of living on the coast? He should have seen the possibility, insisted that they move inland. But Sekate, tucked inside Oura Bay, seemed ideal in all ways – until now.

As it turns out, the protection of the bay would turn against them, funneling the wave toward the village, pressurizing it in the process, like putting your thumb over the end of a hose. It would hit hard. The best he could hope for is that she could either outrun the wave or survive the flood. Both of which he knew were unlikely.

He began to pick up speed, breaking through the dream-state slowness. The throng of villagers running for higher ground shouted at him to turn around. He absolutely would not go without Kasumi. The thickening crowds made passage difficult as he bounced off one person, then another. He forced his way through, the whole time looking desperately for her face, calling her name.

Finally, he spotted her, and she him. They ran toward each other. What Kasumi could not see which Akio had a strikingly clear image of, was a wave, thirty feet high, and closing fast. They finally connected, latching on to each other tightly. Akio watched as the water that had been sucked up into the cresting wave hesitated for an instant, suspended between ebb and flow, before curling over itself and crashing onto the docks a hundred yards away.

In a cave deep in the Himalayan mountains, a monk was roused from his meditation. With great sadness, he stood up, walked across the cave and crossed off the next hash mark on the wall, leaving three remaining vertical lines untouched.

Chapter 13

#998

Sarah left her office armed with a list of all babies born on November 11th. As she projected, the list had nineteen names on it. Eight were girls. She knew she was looking for a boy but she couldn't very well skip over the female babies. That would certainly raise some eyebrows. And besides, she really did believe in her program, even though it was contrived to serve another purpose. With her GPS preset, she grabbed her clipboard and headed to her car. The Jetta was already loaded with baskets decorated with a traditional blue or pink ribbon. Her list was also color coded, with a dot in front of each address indicating gender. The seven houses closest to her location were programmed in. The first house, just two miles from her office, was a boy.

As she pulled up in front of the first house, she was feeling uncomfortably nervous. This was not just a wellness check on the mom. This was a search for a very unique being with the potential to change the world.

She shook her head, trying to refocus on the mundane purpose for her visit. After all, she was here to help others first and foremost. Knocking lightly on the door, she stood back and waited.

A young, tired-looking woman answered the door with a baby in her arms, the little blue hat indicating a male child. Sarah knew it would be a boy, and still, she froze. Her planned speech was completely gone from her conscious mind. She stared at the baby then reached up to feel the medallion beneath her blouse. Nothing unusual. No apparent sign from the gods.

"Can I help you?" the woman asked her.

"Ah, no. I mean yes. Well, really, I'd like to help you." Sarah hit her stride. "I'm from Building Futures. We're a social services agency that works with young mothers. I'm here to do a little outreach, letting you know all the ways we can help you." She offered forward one of the Welcome Baskets with a large blue ribbon draping down from the top. It contained trial sizes of diapers and lotions, along with a few healthy snacks for busy moms.

"I don't need any help, thank you."

"I'm glad to hear that. Maybe someone you know does. I'll just leave this with you as a gift. It has our contact information and brochure. Just in case. Thank you."

The woman accepted the basket and Sarah headed back to the car. This mom appeared to have things under control and Sarah didn't want to spend more time than necessary when she could be continuing her search.

Back in her car, she reached for her clipboard and checked off the first name. Maybe this won't be so bad after all.

She arrived at the next house a few minutes away. This

neighborhood was a little rougher and the houses were in need of repair. She grabbed a blue-ribboned basket and headed to the door. This could be the one.

"Yes?" Another tired mom answered the door. Sarah could hear a baby screaming in the background.

"Hi. My name is Sarah and I'm with Building Futures, a social service agency that focuses on helping new moms. Can I tell you a little about our services?"

"You got a service that can stop a baby from crying?" she tried for sarcastic but only achieved desperate.

"Well, I can say that I have a knack for putting babies to sleep. I'm happy to give it a try and in the meantime, you can look through our Welcome Basket."

Surprisingly, the woman let her in. Sarah wasn't sure how close she needed to be for the medallion to work, so she figured she'd get as close as she could. She handed the basket off to the mom and headed for the bassinet. She picked up the baby and held him close to the medallion. Nothing happened, except that the baby stopped crying as Sarah rocked him gently and cooed him with shhhh shhhh shhhh. She had read somewhere that the sh sound was what babies could hear in the womb.

The mom broke into tears. "Tell me you can stay for two hours," she pleaded.

"No. I'm sorry I can't, but I can stay for a few minutes at least and talk about how we can come back and help you regularly for the next few months. How would that be?"

"Like a gift from heaven."

And so it went for the entire afternoon, a total of seven visits and no messages from the medallion. Sarah was getting discouraged. On the upside, she had identified four families that could use some serious help so she didn't consider the day a loss at all. Helping new mothers just seemed right.

The next two days brought her to the end of her list with no secret messages, no identified Buddha. What happened? Her first thought was that she had done something wrong or missed some trick of the medallion. She ran everything over in her mind again and again. Had this all been a wild goose chase? Her instinct told her no. The monk had been very clear. The child was born three weeks ago, a boy. She took out her day planner and recounted the days since her trek in the mountains. What had she missed? Maybe it was a time-of-day issue? Was it three weeks from the exact moment they talked?

"Oh no!" she hit herself on the forehead. "The time difference!" At the moment she was talking to the monk, it was already the next day in Guam. She quickly allowed for the time zone adjustment. "Let's see, the baby might have been born the day after Nov. 11th. November 12th!" Had she been spinning her wheels for three days? It was the only thing that made sense. She was in a panic. She had to get on this fast. What if something goes sideways before she gets to the little guy? She spun her car around and sped off, back to the Hall of Records.

Chapter 14
#997

Nathan was running late when he arrived at Rosa Parks Middle School, number six on his list, to give his scholarship presentation to the seventh and eighth graders. It was already getting tedious and he was hoping it would bear fruit soon.

"Hello, Principal Lasser. Nice to see you again." He said, extending his hand.

"Welcome back, Nathan. Always happy to see someone who is helping my kids." Dr. Harold Lasser, or Doc Lasser, as the kids called him, was the most well-liked principal Nathan had talked to so far. And he understood why. The man had a knack of putting people at ease, adults and kids alike.

Nathan was eager to get the presentation over with. If this school wasn't it, he had plenty of others to scan. "So, have you told the kids what the assembly is about?"

"No. I just told them it was for something good so they wouldn't worry."

"Thanks for that." Shall we get started?"

“Right this way. The kids are already in the auditorium.”

Nathan and Doc Lasser headed into the assembly hall through a back door and opened onto the side of a small stage. As soon as Nathan stepped out from the wings, he felt a strange sensation in his chest. At first, he thought it was nerves, although he couldn’t understand why. He had plenty of experience talking to large and small groups of all kinds. He adjusted his shoulders and tugged on his suit coat, hoping to shake the feeling but it persisted, right in the center of his chest. Was he having a heart attack? A flash of panic crept. That can’t be. He’s in perfect health. What then? Realization filtered through his thoughts. The sensation was a faint vibration from the medallion. His heart quickened and he tensed with excitement. Doc Lasser noticed the change in Nathan's demeanor.

“You okay, Nathan?” he whispered sideways.

“Yeah, great.” Nathan quickly regained his composure. “Everything is great.”

He rushed through the power point and then launched into an ad lib addendum.

“So, what I'd like everyone to do now it to line up here at the bottom of the stage and, one by one, sign in saying that you want your name to be on the scholarship list.”

Doc Lasser looked over at him, surprised by the unexpected twist.

Nathan shrugged an apology. “New rule. I forgot to mention it. Sorry. The kids have to sign up themselves. We can't do it for them.”

“Okay then,” Doc got on board easily. “Let's start with the front row and then just keep going by row.” He was already orchestrating the process when Nathan sat down at a table with a note pad and pen.

"So," he addressed the first child, "If you want to be on the list, start us off by printing your name here and then your grade." He handed the student a pen and pointed to the first line of the sheet he had quickly created, titled Scholarship Members. The medallion was still vibrating at a low level as the students passed one by one. Nathan chatted it up for a moment with each child just in case the medallion needed a moment to zoom in. Then suddenly, things started ramping up as the next child stepped up to the table. It became so strong that Nathan was worried it might actually be seen moving beneath his shirt. His heart was pounding as he looked up at the boy standing before him.

"Hey there, young man. What's your name?"

"Devon."

"Well, Devon. Would you like some help going to college?"

"Sure. I guess." The truth was that Devon had not considered for a moment that he would be needing a scholarship. He was only in line because there didn't seem to be any way out of it.

"Alright then. Sign right here, Devon." Nathan indicated the next line, leaning over as Devon filled in his name.

"Devon Johnson," Nathan read. "Well, glad to meet you. Will I see you at some of the sports events?"

"Yeah. I guess. Will you be giving out stuff?" Devon was always interested if food was provided.

"We'll probably have a hot dog cart at least, and maybe t-shirts. How does that sound?"

That got Devon's attention. "Sounds great," he said with a little more enthusiasm.

"Then, I'll look forward to seeing you."

Devon turned away before Nathan could continue the

conversation, and headed back to class.

Nathan continued to talk it up with the kids, but his focus was on Devon Johnson now. He could hardly contain himself. He couldn't wait to tell Kate.

Chapter 15

#997

"Wow! That's almost unbelievable. Are you sure? Maybe it was just your imagination." Kate was truly shocked, and a little disappointed perhaps. She was half hoping that this would all blow over and prove to be a fool's errand. Nathan had committed to marriage and family, and this mystery boy was distracting him. She wanted to be supportive, but… If this medallion had, in fact, identified someone, it would prove at least some of the story was true. Still, it seemed a little farfetched and added another responsibility on Nathan.

"Not imagination. This thing was jumping." Nathan had pulled he medallion out from under his shirt and was studying it. "It doesn't look any different though."

She walked across the kitchen to examine it herself. "It does seem to be a little warm," she noticed, "or is that just you?" she teased, putting her hand on his chest.

"Is that how you think of me? A little warm?" He managed to pull her close and kiss her before she squirmed way.

"I have dinner on the stove."

"Oh, yes. And thank you for that. I'm starving." Nathan reached up into the cabinet, retrieved two plates and began setting the table. "What do you think I should do next?" He had been working out different plans in his head all afternoon of how to connect with Devon.

"Well, tell me about him. What does he look like? Is he an athlete or a scholar?"

"He's a dark-skinned kid. At least partly African American by appearance. He didn't strike me as particularly athletic but he's still young, so, hard to say. He did seem interested in the sports events though."

"Okay. What else?"

"His clothes were old, inexpensive and not entirely clean. I only got a moment with him but he seemed like a thoughtful kid, more mature than his age and his peers."

"Oh-oh."

"What do you mean, oh-oh?" Nathan got concerned.

"Well, at the risk of generalizing, kids that grow up in difficult situations often grow up faster."

"Sure. That makes sense. He did ask me if I would be giving things away at these events."

"Bingo. My suggestion is to always have food, even if it's just snacks and juice boxes. And clothing like sweatshirts or sneakers. Socks too."

"Really? Socks?"

"Yeah. Most people don't realize it. The homeless and poor people get lots of clothing from donations, but they don't get underwear and socks unless the shelter buys them new. They usually keep that stuff out of sight and hand them out if someone asks or they clearly see the need."

"Wow. I had no idea. I'll add that to the list. How do you know this stuff?"

"How do you not know? You're marketing to a whole different population now. You better get up on the statistics. Inner city Chicago is one of the poorest places in the country.

"You're right. I've been too busy building the program – getting sponsors, donations, scheduling events, visiting schools. Time to look closer at the kids."

"You probably don't know what a food desert is either." She challenged him.

"Ah, no. Enlighten me." He smiled.

"Cute." She resisted the urge to smile. "In some of the worst areas of the inner city, it's nearly impossible to get fresh food like fruits and vegetables. There's no grocery store within walking distance and most inner-city poor don't have cars. They rarely leave their neighborhood. It's just one of the challenges of good nutrition for these families. That's why school lunch is so important."

"Alright. Alright. I get it. I definitely need to brush up on social issues."

Kate put three bowls on the table. "Fresh vegetables, garlic rice and marinated chicken."

"Wow. No desert here. This is great."

"Well," she smiled at him, "I need to watch what I eat. I'm building a baby you know."

Nathan couldn't imagine being happier.

Chapter 16

#997

It was dark and Devon was getting colder by the minute. He's been kicked out again, in deference to TJ and was walking the streets, looking for a place to be. He ran into some of the older kids on the corner, by an empty playground.

"Hey, D. How'd you like to make a little money tonight?" Biggie asked him.

Devon was a little suspicious of the offer. "Is it illegal?" he asked, which caused a roar of laughter from the other kids.

"No, little man," Biggie chuckled. "Jus' deliverin' a message. Tha's all."

"What I gotta do?" Devon intentionally slipped into street slang even though he hated it. He thought it made people sound stupid, but he didn't want to offend anyone by using uppity English.

"See this here money?"

"Yeah."

"You gotta take it to a house 'round the corner. Tha's it."

“For real?'

“Yeah.”

“I don't gotta pick nothin' up?” It seemed too simple and Devon wanted to be sure there wasn’t more going on.

“Nope. We got someone else going by to pick up a package later. All you gotta do is drop the dough.”

“How much?” Devon was getting interested. He sure could use a few bucks.

“Ha ha ha, little man. I see I got your attention.” Biggie joked, getting chuckles from the others. “How does ten dollars sound?”

Devon tried to play it cool but his heart was racing. Ten dollars! He wondered how many dinners that would buy him. Two, maybe three or maybe a pair of warm socks. “And it's all legal?” He made one last query.

“Sho' it is. I can give money to anyone I want. In a minute I'm gonna give you ten dollars. Nuttin' wrong with that.”

“Okay. Where'd I gotta go?” He was nervous but willing to try it out.

“Okay, my little man. Here's the deal. You go 'round to numba 16 Circle Court. Knock just one time, and I mean just once, on the screen door on the back porch. You got me?” Biggie checked in.

“Yeah. Knock one time on the screen door.”

“A guy is going to let you into the little hallway. He won't let you into the house, just out of sight of the nosy neighbors. When you're inside, give him the money. Tha's it. You got it?”

“I got it. How come I gotta go in?”

“Ah, you're thinkin'. I like that.” Biggie nodded his head in approval. “See, if no one sees money change hands and you don't come out with any merchandise, then there ain't no drug deal. You get it?"

"Yeah."

"Then we got someone to go by later and pick up the package."

"Okay. I got this." Devon sounded more confident than he was.

"Here you go." Biggie handed him a wad of bills wrapped in plain white paper and secured with a rubber band. "Numba 16 Circle Court. Then come straight back here and let me know it's done."

"Got it." Devon shoved the money into his coat pocket and headed down the street.

It was already dark and the streetlights were mostly broken. He'd walked these streets in the dark before, but tonight they seemed more ominous that usual. He knew that what he was doing was just on the edge of bad, but ten dollars was too hard to pass up. He'd try it tonight and if it went as expected, he'd consider it again.

He turned the corner onto Circle Court, eyeing number sixteen. He knew the house already. It's hard to live in the neighborhood and not know where the dealers were. Even the cops knew. He'd always kept his distance, until now.

A wave of adrenalin pumped through him as he walked up to the back porch. Not so much about what might happen to him today but about the road he was starting down. He knew once you were in the 'business' it was impossible to get out. Hopelessness fell over him as he knocked just once. A big man, about thirty or so, came to the door, puffed up his chest and demanded to know what Devon wanted.

A little scared, he stammered, "Biggie told me to come by."

"Oh yeah?"

"Yes, sir." Devon defaulted to good manners. "He told me to give you something." He was careful not to take it out of his pocket.

The large man looked him over, then opened the screen door. "Get in here."

Devon did as he was told entering a small hallway. It was dark and smelled heavily of marijuana.

Once the door was closed, the man barked, "Give me what you got."

Devon reached into his pocket and handed over the bundle. The man stuffed it into his own pocket without looking at it, then stared at a spot somewhere over Devon's head. "You're not the regular boy."

"No, sir."

The man turned to look towards the house then back out over Devon's head. In a quiet voice, the man said, "You seem like a smart kid. Don't get yourself sucked into all this."

"I need the money, sir," Devon whispered back in his own defense.

The man nodded understanding, still not looking at him. "Be careful."

"Yes, sir." Devon let himself out and ran as fast as he could back to Biggie, where he collected his ten dollars and headed for home. It was still early so he would have to wait outside, out of sight, until TJ left, but he didn't care. He didn't want to hang out with Biggie and friends any longer than he had to.

Chapter 17

#998

Sarah's boss had been more than satisfied by the results so far. Eight new clients in three days was a stunning success. Their best marketing strategy had never gotten those kinds of results. So, when Sarah offered to start on the next days' newborns, Rita was all over it. Armed with her second list of babies, Sarah headed out early the next day. Twenty-three names this time. Twelve boys.

She had fine-tuned her delivery by now and felt confident working her way into the homes of strangers. It was surprisingly easy since the culture of Guam was mostly peaceful and trusting. A quality that worked to her advantage.

She grabbed a blue-ribboned basket and headed to the first door. “Good morning,” she greeted the mom who answer her knock. “I'm from Building Futures, a social service agency...”

Before she could finish, the mom was waving her off. “No, thank you, dear. We're all set.”

"Well, at least take this Welcome Basket. It has our contact info and services. If not for you, for someone else." She found most people didn't refuse free stuff, whether they needed it or not.

"Okay. Sure. Thank you."

Sarah was beginning to worry. What if she didn't find the baby in the service area of Building Futures? She wasn't sure she could convince the company to do an island wide sweep. The island wasn't that big but it wasn't that small either. Or what if she'd already visited the house but didn't get close enough to the baby, like at the last stop? She had to believe that the radius of the medallion covered more than just a few feet and that getting to the doorstep would give some indication. And she was starting to feel a little disingenuous, deceitful even, as she knocked on all these doors and lied to the new moms.

Not entirely a lie, she reminded herself as she moved on to the next name on the list and then the next. She decided she could squeeze one more stop for the day into her part-time hours. The last stop was in an affluent area so it was unlikely that they would need much help but it was a blue basket baby so she pushed herself to check it out. Wouldn't it be nice, she thought, if the baby was born into a nice, stable home that could provide the best of life?

As she pulled up in front of the home of Marion and Chris Rivera, she felt a slight sensation in her chest. She thought it was surprising that she was a little nervous. She had already visited more than thirty homes. This was obviously a very wealthy neighborhood, and, truth be told, rich people intimidated her a little. She felt much more at home with the urban poor. As she sat in her car, she took a deep breath trying to regain her composure. No luck. Then she placed her hands on her chest hoping to quell the nerves. Suddenly, it was all clear. She wasn't nervous at all! It was the medallion!

"Oh my god, oh my god, oh my god! It's doing something," she whispered to herself. "Okay, calm down. Calm down." More deep breaths eased the initial shock. "So, this is it? This is the house?" When she pulled the medallion out of her blouse, it stopped vibrating. She remembered the monk's words. Wear it on your skin. It draws power from your energy field and the energy emitted by the Buddha child. When she tucked the medallion back onto her skin, it resumed its gentle buzzing.

She was almost trembling when she walked up to the door. The closer she got to the house the stronger the response from the necklace. She could hardly contain herself as she rang the bell.

A well-dressed woman came to the door, a stunningly clean burping cloth draped over her shoulder. "Yes, can I help you?"

"Ah, yes, I hope so." Fortunately, she had had lots of practice delivering the opening remarks. "My name is Sarah and I'm from Building Futures, a social services organization focusing on helping new moms."

"Yes, I'm familiar with your agency," the mom replied.

"You are?" This pulled Sarah out of her usual routine. "Oh, how is that? Have you used us before?" It was obviously a stupid question considering the neighborhood.

The woman graciously smiled. "No, but I'm on the board of A New Life Church and we refer people to you when we have someone in need."

"Oh, that's so great. Thank you for that." Sarah was stumbling for what to say next. She wanted desperately to keep the conversation going. "Is there any way I might help you? I understand you might not be in need of our services but is there anything else you need?" She was babbling. She knew it. "How is your new baby? The only information I have is that he's a boy."

"He is a boy. James Lee. And he's a constant delight." His mother beamed a huge smile then blushed. "I must sound like a naive young mother who thinks her baby is perfect. But, well, he really is. Would you like see for yourself?"

That was music to Sarah's ears. "Yes. I'd love to. I love babies. There's so precious."

"Come on in. By the way, I'm Marion."

"It's a pleasure to meet you – and your son." Sarah followed Marion into the living room where a tiny baby lay swaddled in a fluffy blue blanket resting in a small electric swing, rocking gently back and forth to soft classical music. She caught her breath when she laid eyes on him. The medallion was nearly jumping out of her blouse. Her heart was beating a mile a minute. He was the most beautiful baby she had ever seen. Okay, maybe she was a little biased knowing this small being could be the next Buddha, fulfilling the promise of transformation for the human race. But still...

"Hey, little one," she cooed to him, "Someday you're going to save the world." She hadn't realized she said it out loud until Marion commented on it.

"Well, I don't know about saving the world. We just hope he grows up to be happy and healthy."

"Yes. Of course," Sarah stammered. "I get a little carried away."

"You know, the one thing we do need is a nanny, just part time. Unfortunately, I'll have to go back to work sooner or later, at least for a few hours a day. You wouldn't happen to know anyone, would you?"

Sarah couldn't believe her ears. Could this get any more perfect? “Well, if I'm not speaking out of turn, I'd love to be considered for the job. I'm only part time at Building Futures and I'm sure they can be flexible. What hours were you thinking?”

“I was thinking afternoons. Starting in a few weeks.”

“Please consider me. I can get you my resume and as many references as you like. I'm a licensed social worker with a focus on early childhood development. It's a perfect match.”

“Fine, Sarah,” Marion smiled at her. “As long as your credentials prove out, you've got the job.”

“Oh, they will. You'll see. Everything is in perfect order.” She turned to the baby. “Oh, baby James Lee, it looks like we might be spending a lot of time together.” She gazed at the baby as if there were nothing more amazing in the whole world.

Marion couldn't be sure, but it looked like James Lee gave Sarah the slightest smile.

Chapter 18

#997

The Guiding Light of the Word Temple, on West Wellington Boulevard in Chicago, was founded in 1875 to serve the hundreds of Chinese workers who remained in the area after the transcontinental railroad line was completed. Its current mission, according to their website, was to support a thriving Buddhist community that reflected the melting pot of America. People from all walks of life, all races and ages, came together at its many weekly meditation programs in search of peace and understanding. A small monastic order, led by Temple Master Chen Tse Lu, maintained the property and supported the congregation.

This week, when Master Chen received a request to report to the home office in Katmandu, the chatter among the monastic community could not be stopped. Something big must be in the pipeline. Maybe the Master is being reassigned, or called to a different mission. Maybe a new leader is going to be promoted from within.

Brother Chen tried to slow the gossip. "I'm sure it's just an administrative update. I'll be back in a week or so. Please refrain from all these speculations." But the sudden nature of the call had sparked curiosity even in him. What could be so important as to call him half way around the world? Could it be a Buddha? He blew it off as being highly unlikely, virtually impossible. But still…would he finally be asked to answer the most divine call of all? Or was the meeting purely a strategy session in the worst-case scenario, that no remaining Buddha reaches the ultimate point of understanding – enlightenment? His mind was embarrassingly busy as he packed for the journey.

Headquarters for The Guiding Light Foundation was a modest building at the foot of the Himalayas. Brother Chen paused to appreciate its simplicity. Eight sides, corresponding to the Eightfold Path of Buddhism, were made of plain white stucco, with a small window in the center of each wall. A red tile roof gave it an almost Mediterranean flavor except for the slight curve of the classic pagoda style. Brother Chen thought it an odd structure that stood out among the flat roofed adobe buildings nearby. Maybe that was the point.

Its simple architecture belied the breadth of its reach. The Foundation's stated mission was the proliferation of Buddhist teachings. From a small beginning, it had grown to an international organization. Today, it boasted outposts in eighty-seven countries on all continents. Unbeknownst to all but a few, the Foundation had an underlying purpose. Beneath its large umbrella, a select group of religious leaders received very special training.

Established by the Dali Lama 2,000 years ago, the task of this covert team of clergy was to find the next Buddha and monitor his or her development. When the time came, they stepped in to provide training in all aspects of divine knowledge. The secret order could mobilize a teacher almost instantly to anywhere in the world.

Brother Chen hadn't been back here since he received his own elite training twenty-seven years ago. It hadn't changed much, he thought, except for the expected maintenance, fresh paint, new windows, landscaping. He wondered how many others had been here since then. He was loosely in touch with a few other "graduates" but, scattered all over the world, they mostly kept to themselves. The shroud of secrecy allowed for very little contact outside the order. He had no family and few friends. Some days he wondered if the isolation was worth it. After all, what were the odds he would ever be called up for the task for which he was trained?

Two thousand years ago, when life was simpler, identifying those chosen to Buddhahood was relatively easy. Buddhist communities were eager to aid these gifted children. Many achieved enlightenment quietly and went on to live monastic lives. But as the global population grew, Buddhas were often overlooked or went unidentified, some dying before their training could even begin. Another unforeseen problem arose when Buddhas started appearing in other religious traditions. To keep up with the changing needs, this once-tiny team of Buddhist monastics grew to include all of the world's major religions, a super-select multicultural association devoted to the enlightenment of the chosen ones. They called themselves The Knowledge Keepers, preserving the most powerful teachings ever known to humanity, including the secrets of alchemy and immortality. Each enlightened Buddha would bring their own essence to this divine knowledge, resulting in an increasingly powerful leader to guide the transformation of mankind into the new age.

Knowledge Keepers, such as Brother Chen, were secretly embedded into religious communities all over the world. They had no idea if they would ever be called to the task, but they, and their predecessors, had been at the ready for centuries. They all knew time was running out in regards to the last Buddha, but only a few knew how close they were.

Chen checked in at the temple office.

"Yes. Brother Chen Tse Lu. You are expected. Please make yourself comfortable in the dormitory, room 12."

"It there some kind of meeting scheduled? I was barely given any information."

"There are instructions and supplies in your room."

Chen resisted the urge to ask the next logical question. What supplies? The answer came shortly when he opened the door to his room to find a backpack, fully loaded, with a bedroll strapped to the top.

The room was small, just big enough for a twin cot and a small nightstand. The walls were bare except for the image of the Buddha hanging at the foot of the bed. A tented note card rested on the nightstand.

Brother Sulee will come for you at 6 am with further instructions.

Chen's assent to the cave was arduous. Sulee had walked the first three miles with him in silence. Then directed him up the next path. His light bedroll and supplies hadn't felt heavy when he left the village. Now, four hours into the walk, the straps were uncomfortable on his shoulders, the load slowing him down. Admittedly, he was not a young man, turning the corner on fifty-eight earlier this year, but he thought he would fare better than this. Perhaps city life had made him a little soft, he wondered. Either way, he hoped the walk down would be easier. He was sure sleeping on the floor of a cave wasn't going to help.

He entered the outer cave with the greatest of reverence, gently dropping his pack. Retrieving his water, he refreshed himself as he looked around. He inhaled deeply the familiar aroma of incense. Deeper into this cave sat the greatest being he knew of – Grand Master Gathnadi, head of the Knowledge Keepers. There had never been any other leader, as far as anyone knew. Rumor had it that the monk was over two thousand years old. Now, Brother Chen was going to meet him. He centered himself, hands pressed together over his heart and breathing deeply before continuing further back.

Chen spotted the old master as soon as he entered the inner sanctum. The monk sat perfectly still, eyes closed. Brother Chen immediately lowered himself to the straw mat covering the dirt floor, and prostrated before him, waiting acknowledgement.

"Please rise, Brother Chen Tse Lu. Be seated that we may talk," the old monk instructed.

Slowly, Brother Chen rose and seated himself, lotus style, on the small pile of folded blankets.

Placing his palms together in front of his chest he bowed from his seat. "Master, I present myself humbly before you. Ask anything, that I might be of service."

"Brother Chen, as you might suspect, the time is late for our task of bringing the sacred teaching to the next Buddha."

"There is some talk of it, yes, Master." Brother Chen noticed for the first time the hash marks on the wall. Gasping, he blurted out, "Master! Is this the count?"

"Yes. We are currently at 999. Three are alive. One yet to be born."

The monk looked stricken. "I had no idea. This is dire."

"Perhaps, perhaps not. We have taken extraordinary measures to ensure the safety of these souls."

"Master, how can I possibly serve you?"

"Number nine hundred ninety-seven lives in Chicago."

Brother Chen gasped again. Wide-eyed, he stammered, "Certainly there is a mistake." Even though he had considered the possibility ever since his arrival at the Guiding Light of the World Temple ten years ago, the reality of such a sacred soul being born in Chicago seemed so remote as to be absurd.

"There is no mistake."

They both sat in silence while Brother Chen digested this information.

When he had regained his monastic composure, he spoke. "How can I serve?"

"We have enlisted the aid of an American to locate him. At that time, he will reach out to you."

"Very well," nodded Brother Chen.

"I assume you are prepared to begin his training at any time?"

"Without hesitation, Master. I have lived for this moment. I am ready."

Chapter 19

#997

Nathan had driven by The Guiding Light of the World Temple hundreds of times. It was one of his alternate routes to work if traffic got jammed up on Jefferson Boulevard. Now, he spent the extra minutes each morning intentionally driving by, wondering. He had never been inside. Never even seen any activity from the outside. The monk had suggested that he become familiar with the community as soon as possible, but Nathan had been putting it off. Besides being busy tracking down and connecting with Devon, he had an unexplainable hesitation about it. What if Devon didn't want to be a Buddhist? The monk had said that the previous Buddhas had come from all disciplines. Nathan had been raised Methodist, although it didn't mean much in his life at the moment. Did Devon's family have any particular affiliation? Even if they had no religion at all, Buddhism would be a hard sell.

Pushing past the Methodist taboo against any alternate ideology, he finally checked the temple's website for programs or activities. There was a Newcomers' Orientation this coming Saturday.

Kate had surprisingly agreed to attend.

"Sure. Why wouldn't I?" she asked, rubbing the small bump appearing on her belly.

"Well, how about because your family is pretty staunchly Jewish?"

"So? If you hadn't noticed, I make up my own mind about that sort of thing. We've had lots of conversations about this, Nathan. What's the big deal?"

"I don't know. Our talks have been mostly a Christian-Jewish dialog with a smattering of Agnosticism and a pinch of Humanism. We've never really considered the Eastern teachings."

"So, maybe it's time?"

"Maybe it is."

They stood on the steps to the temple wondering what the protocol was. Do they knock? Ring a bell? Or is it like church and you just go in. While they were considering the options, a man walked by them, heading in through the main doors.

When he noticed their hesitation, he smiled warmly and asked, "Good morning. Can I help you?" He was wearing a shawl similar to ones Nathan had seen many times in Nepal.

"Yes," Kate responded. "We're here for the Newcomers meeting."

"Oh, right this way. I'll be happy to show you."

Nathan pulled a shawl out of his satchel. "Should I wear this?"

"Oh, that's beautiful. Yes, by all means, wear it if you like. A lot of us have them." He indicated his own draped around his neck.

Kate, sensitive to cultural issues, asked, “Can I wear my Jewish shawl? We're not sure what's customary and I don't want to offend anyone.”

“Nonsense. We are very accommodating here. No worries. And yes, please wear your shawl if you like. We believe that shawls carry the energy of all the prayers we've made while wearing them. The older the better.”

Kate took her shawl out of a small canvas tote bag and draped it over her shoulders while Nathan did the same.

“This looks quite authentic,” the man said gesturing to Nathan's shawl. “Did you get it here?”

“No, I spent some time in Nepal this summer and picked it up there.” The shawl was a gift from the monk upon his departure. It had multicolored stripes going the long way with a hint of gold thread running opposite.

“How nice for you. Most of us hope to make that pilgrimage in our lifetime.”

“Well, I certainly recommend it,” Nathan replied. But he didn't want this conversation to go any further so he started walking up the remainder of the stairs as he spoke, followed by Kate and the gentleman. “Is this a busy place? I never see much going on.”

“Yes, quite busy. We have programs every morning and again in the evening a few nights a week. And on the weekends of course. You’re in for a treat today. Our senior monk, Brother Chen, recently took over running the intro programs personally.”

“Who usually does them?” Kate inquired.

“Usually, it's a novice monk. The idea being that as you teach, you learn. But for some reason Brother Chen has chosen to take over the task himself.”

They continued into the building, with their escort

leading the way down a hallway to the right, to a small temple room with pillows set up on the floor in a circle. A few chairs were against the wall, presumably as options if needed. There were a few people already seated on the floor.

The man waved them in, “Take a seat anywhere you like. Brother Chen will be in shortly.”

“Thank you,” Kate and Nathan both replied.

They entered the room and automatically took positions on the floor. The room was simple in some ways, white walls, minimal décor, simple furnishings, except for a large platform about the size and height of a card table centered against the wall in the front of the room. Upon it was a golden statue of the Buddha, decorated with lots of fresh flowers and strands of beads. Flags of various colors hung behind it on the wall, each one detailed with a symbol outlined in gold. Several layers of silk covered the platform, in all colors and prints. It was a stark contradiction to the rest of the room. Off to one side was a raised platform, maybe the height of a standard step, carpeted and topped with a pillow. Everyone was silent.

A few more people trickled in and took seats on the floor. At exactly the top of the hour, an older gentleman entered the room. Presumably, Brother Chen, based on the simple dark red robes and shaved head. He walked to the front of the room and stood beside the Buddha.

“Welcome, everyone.” He took a moment to survey the attendees, scanning each face, starting from one side of the room and working his way around. When he passed over Nathan, he hesitated for the briefest of moments before continuing his observations.

“My name is Brother Chen. I'm going to tell you a little about Buddhism today. Then we will meditate for only a very brief time and then I will answer any and all questions you might have."

Brother Chen took them through the program with ease and, true to his word, answered all questions. Nathan and Kate sat quietly throughout the presentation.

In closing, Brother Chen invited everyone to greet him as they left. "I like to say a personal welcome to everyone so please stop and say hello before you leave." With that, he bowed to the group and took up a place at the door.

Kate and Nathan got in line with the others. As he shook hands with Brother Chen, the monk leaned closer to him. "That's a lovely shawl. You got in Nepal, yes?"

"Yes. As a matter of fact, I did. In a small bazaar." Nathan evaded.

"The pattern is very unique. It is not sold in any market. It was a gift. Yes?"

Embarrassed to be caught in his lie, Nathan stuttered a bit. "Well, yes, actually it was."

Leaning in a little closer, the monk almost whispered, "Please stay and we can talk about Nepal."

"Certainly." Nathan released the monk's hand and stepped away. Brother Chen greeted Kate as well and motioned that she should wait with Nathan. The monk proceeded to greet each remaining attendee and welcome them to the center, encouraging them to return for a program soon.

When the last visitor had gone, he turned to Nathan and Kate.

"Welcome. You must be Nathan," Brother Chen began. "And who is the lady you bring with you?"

Again, Nathan was caught off guard. "Oh, I'm sorry. Ah, this is my girlfri... ah, fiancé, Kate."

"It is a pleasure to meet you both. I have been waiting for you." Brother Chen turned and closed the door, then motioned to the chairs in the back of the room. "Please, sit and let us talk."

Brother Chen moved three chairs out from the wall, circling them into a group.

"I don't know why I'm surprised that you know who I am considering recent events."

"Yes," the monk nodded. "I was made aware of your mission recently and I want to start by saying how grateful I am for your assistance. Have you located our charge?"

"As a matter..."

"Wait a minute," Kate interrupted. "How do we know you're the one we're supposed to be talking to?"

"Kate! What are you saying?"

"I'm just saying that this is a very sensitive project. How do we know he's the right one to be talking to? He could be anyone or worse, someone who has ulterior motives."

"Kate!" Nathan chastised her. Then turned to the monk. "I'm really sorry. She's a skeptic by nature," then, after a quick reflection, "but she does have a point." He waited for the monk's reply.

"Of course. My apologies. Let me explain. I just returned from Nepal, from a small village deep in the highlands, off the beaten trail. While there, I visited a monk, isolated even higher up in a cave in the mountainside. On the wall of the cave were marks hashed out in coal. Nine hundred and ninety-nine of them. Does that suffice?"

Nathan and Kate looked at each other. Neither voiced any concern. "Okay," Nathan said, "You have our attention."

"Thank you for being cautious," Brother Chen acknowledged. "Have you found the boy?"

"Yes," Nathan responded with a slight sense of pride at the accomplishment.

The monk gasped. "That's amazing. However did you do it?"

"Well, I had to make a lot of promises that I'm hoping the temple can back me up with."

"Yes, Yes. Of course. Anything you need."

"I need you to sponsor a basketball team."

"Oh."

The look of surprise on the monk's face was priceless, causing both Nathan and Kate to break out into a soft chuckle.

"Okay." Brother Chen recovered with a smile of his own. "Tell me how I do that."

Nathan and Kate filled Brother Chen in on the location of Devon and the scheme Nathan had put in play through his work. Brother Chen heartily agreed to do whatever it takes to support this boy.

"There is one more thing," Nathan hedged a bit. He wasn't sure quite how to bring this up.

"Yes, go on," Brother Chen encouraged him.

"I'm not sure what religious affiliation Devon or his family might have. It could be difficult to get him here at all, let alone for any ongoing teachings."

"Not a problem," the monk replied immediately. "We are prepared to honor any spiritual needs."

"You mean you'll train him in any tradition?" Kate asked a little surprised.

"The road to enlightenment is varied, Kate, but ultimately the destination is the same. We are able to accommodate any path. If you tell me what you need, we will supply the teacher."

“Wow. That's quite a network,” Nathan commented. His mind was clicking away, wondering how extensive this select group must be.

“We manage,” was all Brother Chen had to say on the subject.

Recognizing the finality of the remark, Nathan made plans to meet with Brother Chen weekly for updates. They exchanged contact information and headed home.

Chapter 20

#999

Leo was chastising himself for biting off more than he could chew. But wait, he didn't bite this off. It was dumped on him. Who would have thought that a solitary walk through the mountains would have landed him in the middle of some kind of global transformation into a higher something something? Maybe he shouldn't have picked the land of Shangri La to have a midlife crisis.

In his own defense, the monk hadn't given him much choice. "You need you to find the next Buddha child, born in New York City, in order to save the human race from extinction."

What was he supposed to say? Go jump in a lake? You got the wrong guy? What?

So here he was, forty-something, okay, forty-seven, trying to find a holy needle in an unholy haystack.

"Jeez," he shook his head.

"What's the matter with you?"

He had almost forgotten Vince was sitting beside him at the counter of the West Side Diner, having breakfast. True to its name, it had posters of West Side Story adorning the walls and was located just two blocks from the theater where the musical debuted on Broadway in 1957.

"Nothing. What's the matter with you?" he barked back. They both stared forward, alternately studying their breakfast and watching the cook put up orders.

"You know, you haven't been the same since you went looking for yourself," Vince used air quotes for emphasis "in Nepal."

Leo saw the gesture out of the corner of his eye. "Shut up, Vince. You couldn't find your own ass with both hands."

"Maybe not. So, it's a good thing Carla locates it for me on a regular basis."

Leo turned his head to see Vince, staring straight ahead with a sheepish grin turning up the corners of his mouth.

Leo broke from his brooding mood, shaking his head and chuckling. "And it's a good thing. Nobody else would bother."

Friends since high school, Vince had been there for Leo through the best of times and the worst of times, literally. The former as Best Man at his wedding, the latter standing at his side as he buried his wife six months ago. No one can ever imagine the devastation of that loss. His entire future ripped away by a freak traffic accident. No one's fault. It just happened. And in a moment, his life as he knew it was over.

Leo had been at the same job, insurance adjuster, for fifteen years and they were kind enough to give him as much time as he needed to pull things together. When, after three months, it became clear that he wasn't pulling anything together, they gave him the choice of returning or resigning.

Given those options, he shocked everyone by quitting.

"You should never have left that job, Lee. What are you going to do now? Go for walks all over the world?"

Vince was the only one who called him Lee, a nickname since childhood. It was comforting to hear it.

Leo felt for the medallion that hung around his neck. It had a Buddha on one side and a Sanskrit symbol on the other. It hung on the same chain as his cross and a medal of the Blessed Mother. He wasn't all that religious, really, but the charms had a certain cultural comfort that he couldn't explain.

"I know you think I'm crazy, but that part of my life died with Lanie. I just have to figure out what's next. And I have that insurance payout to keep me off the streets for a while." He'd been debating telling Vince about the monk in the cave. Vince already thought he was crazy so there wasn't much to lose. He eased into the topic.

"Something did happen to me in Nepal, you know," Leo said.

"Yeah. I know. When are you going to tell me about it?"

"You probably won't believe me."

"Probably not."

Leo hesitated.

Vince turned to him. "Look. Eventually you're going to tell me. You know you are. So just do it and save us both some time."

Leo looked down at his coffee then took on one of those distance stares while he spoke.

"I met a monk."

"Dude. Really? A monk?" Vince started razzing him.

"Do you want to hear it or not?" Leo looked him straight in the eyes.

"Okay. Sorry. Go."

He resumed his gaze as he went on. “I met a monk in a cave in the middle of nowhere. He told me about a Buddhist tradition of 1000 Buddhas and that the last one would save humanity from itself.”

“Okay.” Vince was listening sincerely now.

“He told me that one of them had just been born in New York City, a baby girl, and that I had to find her.”

“You're kidding?” Vince was back to mockery.

This time Leo was undeterred. “He gave me a medallion that is supposed to do something when I find her.”

“You're serious?”

“Yeah.”

“And you believe him?”

“Yeah.”

Vince was dumbfounded. “What else did he tell you?”

“That she was born on December 13th.”

“This year? Just a few weeks ago?”

“Yeah.”

“Okay. What else?”

“That's it.”

“What! Your secret mission is to find a girl baby in New York City! You have officially lost your mind?” Vince was getting worked up now. “What makes you think that this monk isn't just some nut-job hiding out in a cave with his own delusions?”

“Look. I just know. And I'm not going to justify it to you.”

“Okay. Okay.” Vince tried to sound apologetic. “But you have to know, this is coming out of left field for me.”

“I know.”

“And you know this is ridiculous, right? Like, how are you supposed to find a baby girl in this city, no matter how special she is? Do you know how many babies are born here every day?"

"A little over eight hundred, give or take. I'm figuring, statistically, half of them are girls."

"Okay, so big deal. You looked it up online. You still have to find them."

"You'd be surprised at how easy it is."

"Oh my god! You've found her?" Vince's eyes were nearly popping out of his head.

"No. Not yet. But I got a list of all the babies born in the city on December 13th."

"How the hell did you get that?"

"It's pretty easy, really. Just go to the Hall of Records and ask."

"Leo, you're scaring me. You know this sounds a lot like stalking, right?"

"Yeah."

"Which is illegal, right?"

"I know, Vince. I know. Don't you get it?" Leo's patience was wearing thin. "I know this is crazy and still I have to do it. I can't explain."

Vince took a deep breath while he figured out what to say next. "What are you going to do even if you find this girl?"

"I don't know."

"Oh, this is great. This is just great." Vince ran his hands through his hair thick dark hair. "All I can say is I'll visit you in the big house or in the nut house, whichever way it goes."

"I was hoping you'd help me."

Vince immediately held his hands up and shook his head. "Oh no, no and no-o-o-o. This is your walk in the mountains, not mine."

"Really? After all we've been through, that's all you got

for me?"

They sat at the counter in silence, staring forward, watching the cook set up orders.

"Lee, how do you know this guy in the cave wasn't just crazy?"

"All I can say is that I know. In my heart of hearts, I know."

"Are you sure it's not just your broken heart talking?"

Leo took a deep breath in, calming his anger at the remark. He'd considered the possibility himself but hearing the accusation from Vince stung a bit.

"Look. I know what I know. And I'm not going to do anything crazy. I'm just taking this thing one step at a time. Hell, I didn't think I'd get this far."

Vince waited a long time before responding. "I guess someone's got to bail you out of jail."

Chapter 21

#998

Sarah had just tucked James Lee into his crib for his afternoon nap when she heard Marion come home from work. She turned on the baby monitor and quietly closed the nursery door before heading downstairs.

"Hello, Marion," she said softly. "I just put him down. Did you need anything else?"

She had been just two weeks working as a nanny for baby James Lee, but her ease with the family had developed quickly and the daily routine was already familiar. She would head out whenever Marion or Chris got home unless there was additional assistance needed.

"I'd like to talk to you for a few minutes if you have the time?" Marion was putting her purse down and hanging up her coat.

Sarah had a moment of panic. "Sure. Is anything wrong?"

Marion sensed Sarah's distress. "Not at all. I want to talk about some extra hours. That's all."

Sarah exhaled. “Oh, sure. What’s up?”

“Chris and I are talking with the priest at St. Barbara’s about James’ baptism.”

“What?”

She had been so caught up in the new job and the tiny baby that it never crossed her mind that the baby wouldn't be Buddhist. It was obvious now. The family was clearly Catholic.

Sarah tried to cover her surprise. “What does that have to do with me?”

“We’d like you to help out on that day. There’ll probably be a lot of people here and we thought we could use you to keep tabs on James while we keep an eye on the guests.”

“Oh, sure thing. I’d love to.”

What should she do? In her flurry of activity, she had put off contacting the local Buddhist temple. Now she was close to panic.

“Sarah, are you okay? You look a little distracted. It’s okay to say no. We won’t be mad.”

“Oh, no. It’s not anything like that.” She forced a laugh. “I’ll just have to make sure my schedule is clear. When will it be?”

“We don’t know for sure yet but not till after the holidays.”

“Great. Yeah. Just let me know.” Sarah grabbed her coat and purse and headed for the door. “See you tomorrow.”

She tried to calm herself down when she got to her car. The baby is going to be Catholic. What does that mean? Is that a problem? She considered for a split second taking the baby and running, but on an island five miles long and two miles wide, well... She had to talk to the local monk. Now.

In a near panic, she blasted into the local Buddhist temple insisting to see the person in charge. She was ushered into a meditation room and encouraged to sit quietly for a few minutes while the monk was located.

She jumped out of her chair when a youngish man entered the room wearing dark red robes.

"You don't understand, this baby is one of the thousand. I know it."

"I understand your concern, Miss Sarah," Brother Bensi was saying. "But the Thousand Buddha story is more of a folktale, a fable. Like many other end-of-times stories, it is more allegorical than literal, an invitation for mankind to change his ways or suffer the consequence."

"But the monk in Nepal gave me this." She pulled the medallion out of her blouse without removing it from her neck. "He said it was special."

The monk inspected it causally for a moment. "Miss Sarah." His use of her name was starting to sound condescending. "Trinkets like this can be purchased at any bazaar all over Asia. I fear you have been duped."

Sarah was stunned. What was he saying? Had this all been a hoax? She knew the absurdity of her story. She had questioned it herself many times. But surely, she had talked to the monk in the cave. She didn't make that up, did she? The medallion had trembled, hadn't it? Now that she thought about it, she hadn't felt it recently. Her head was spinning. She was beginning to feel foolishly naive.

"Yes. I'm sure your right." She got up to leave. "Forget I said anything. Just my overactive imagination."

"Perhaps, but do come back if you have any further questions."

"Yes. Of course. Thank you," she called over her shoulder as she darted out the door.

Sarah drove away, frantically trying to make the pieces fit. Was Brother Bensi right? Was she duped? If so, what was the end game? It all seemed so real, not a flicker of doubt, no hazy memories, certainly no alcohol or drugs involved in the trip. Maybe the mystical nature of the mountains and the isolation had played tricks on her.

After a restless night's sleep, she was no less confused than before. She started to wonder if she was competent to care for this infant even assuming none of it was true and James Lee was just an ordinary baby. But as she pulled up in front of the Rivera house for her afternoon shift, she felt the familiar buzz in her chest. She caught her breath. "Oh my God, it's true." She heaved a huge sigh of relief, letting tears seep out the corners of her eyes. Why did the monk steer her off course? He acted like he didn't know anything about the sanctuary in the cave. Then, it occurred to her that maybe he didn't.

Brother Bensi had been quick to discount the story, but the more he thought about it, the more he wondered if any of it were true. He mulled it over for a while and then called his mentor and friend, Brother Saaling at the regional headquarters in Singapore.

Saaling didn't give it much credence. "I'm sure it's nothing, but I'll check it out anyway. No need to bother with it again."

It had been a short conversation. Saaling had been unconcerned, and his instruction had been clear. Leave it alone. So, Bensi let it slip from his mind, carrying on with his regular duties. Two days later he was inexplicably reassigned to a monastery 100 miles west of Shanghai.

Chapter 22

#997

The Temple Monks were playing the Clippers, a team sponsored by a local barber shop, and the only team with a better record. It was expected to be a close game. Brother Chen had shown up as usual. He was seated in the bleachers with Nathan and a handful of parents who had time to attend.

"I'm not sure we're getting anywhere with him," Nathan said.

"Not to worry," replied Brother Chen. "This requires great patience. There is no fast solution."

"I'm worried we'll lose him, you know. That he'll get swallowed up by the city."

"We will follow him as long as it takes. And – I have a plan." The monk smiled while not taking his eyes off the game.

"Oh, really. Do tell."

When the game was over, Nathan and Brother Chen went

down to congratulate the team on a good game, but not a win.

"Great game, boys. Huge effort there at the end," Nathan was saying.

"And hamburgers are on the grill out in the parking lot with Sister Pat," Chen added. "Family is welcome too."

The boys all headed to the door.

"Hold up, Devon," Nathan called.

He reluctantly turned around and headed back.

"What? Did I do something wrong?"

"No. Of course not. Nothing like that. Brother Chen has something you might be interested in.

"Hello, Devon. Nice game," Brother Chen said.

"Thanks." Looking down, he kicked at the air with his foot. He always felt a little weird around Brother Chen, like there was some unspoken expectation. Maybe the monk was like his teachers, thinking that he was something special. Whatever it was, Devon was starting to look up to him more than anyone else he had ever known.

"But it doesn't look like you really love the game, not like some of the other kids."

"It's okay, I guess."

"Well, I've been thinking. I need a little help around the temple. Nathan tells me that you've been assisting him with some of the setup for various events. I was wondering if you would like to take on a small job, like a regular part-time position."

"Maybe." Devon played it cool, not wanting to appear too needy. "What is it?"

"Various odd jobs, yardwork and some general cleaning. I'm thinking every day after school for an hour or two, if you can do it. It includes dinner at the Temple Cafe. And you can do some of your homework there if you like. It's pretty quiet as you can imagine and we have great internet."

The offer was hard to believe and equally hard to turn down, but Devon hedged. "I'll need to check with my mom."

"Yes. Of course. She can call me if she likes."

"She probably won't," Devon said without thinking, then added, "She's busy a lot."

"No problem. Just let me know. You can call me here." Brother Chen handed him a business card for the Temple, "Or text."

"Sure."

Devon headed back to the neighborhood. He wanted this job, but it wasn't his mother he was worried about. He'd been running money for Biggie twice a week. He was trying to figure out if he could do both, running for Biggie and the job at the temple. It didn't work no matter how he figured it. The truth was, he didn't want to run for Biggie, but he needed the money. Now there was an option. For the first time Devon could see the tiniest glimmer of light in his otherwise dark life. He decided to ask the man at the house. After all these weeks, he still didn't know his name, but they had become strange friends during their brief hallway chats. Each time, Devon stayed for a minute or two in case someone saw him going in, so it didn't look too much like a drop-off. Even with their brief encounters, the man was always kind, asking him about school and how he was doing.

The process for the run was that Devon would find Biggie every afternoon and, if there was a need, Devon delivered the cash.

"Hey, Biggie," Devon said as he approached a small group of older boys standing on the street.

"Hey little man. Perfect timing. I got something for ya."

"Yeah?" Already this didn't sound like the usual and Devon's radar was up.

"Yeah. I need you to drop off and pick up."

Devon tried desperately to play it cool. "No drugs, Biggie. You know that. I'm not runnin' drugs."

"No, no, no. I get it. Chill. It's not like that. I need you to drop off as usual, then go to a second house and pick up some cash."

"That's all?'

"Yeah. I swear. That's all."

If nothing else, Biggie hadn't lied to him, so far as he knew anyway.

"Okay. Tell me."

Biggie laid out the instructions, handed Devon a wad of cash, and sent him on his way.

When he arrived at the first stop, the man let him in as usual.

"Hey D." The man used the nickname Biggie had given Devon early on.

"Hey," Devon replied as he handed him the money.

The man sensed something immediately. His back got stiff and straight and he leaned in to Devon. "Is someone out there? Is there a problem?"

"No. No," he reassured him.

The man eased a bit. "Then what's up?"

Devon hesitated a moment. "I want to stop running."

The man looked at him a for a long moment. "Is that right?"

"Yes, sir. I got a job, afternoons."

"Hm."

"I'm scared."

"Hm."

The man didn't say anything for a long time, but he had that look, like his brain was working. He looked to the hallway door that led to the house, then back at Devon. Turning his back to the door, he leaned over, close to Devon's ear. In a low voice, he said, "You tell Biggie you got something next week and you can't run for him. Make up something good that he can't talk you out of. Detention maybe. That'll make him happy, if he thinks you're getting into trouble. You understand?"

"Yes, sir."

"In the meantime, he'll have to get someone else, making it easier for you to work your way out. You understand?" the man asked again.

"Yes, sir."

"I want to see you back here in a week. You can't just disappear. Biggie will come looking for you."

"Yes, sir."

Devon shifted on his feet nervously.

"D? Is there something else?"

"I got another stop today."

"Really?" the man asked, standing up straight again and looking down at Devon. "What's that?"

"I go three blocks down and pick up some other money."

The man continued to look down at him, thinking. "Okay, boy. Do what you're told. Go."

Devon left the hallway feeling a mix of relief and fear. He made his next stop, then headed back to Biggie, who was hanging with the usual posse.

"Everything go okay?" Biggie asked.

"Yeah. No problem." He handed over the cash.

"Sweet. Good job."

Devon mustered up all his courage. "But I got a problem

next week."

The older boys stopped what they were doing and looked at Devon.

"Yeah?" Biggie took a step toward him and got in his face. "What you got that's more important than this?"

Devon backed a step away. He tried not to stammer. "I got detention. All week."

"Seriously, man?" Biggie seemed surprised. "Fo' what?"

"I got into a fight."

"Really?" Biggie was smiling now. "Did you beat his ass good?"

Devon picked up on the tone. "Yeah. I did," he smiled, feigning modesty. "But now I'm in trouble."

The other boys starting laughing and fist-pumping the air. "Yeah, man. You go."

"Good job, little man." He gave him a teasing shove. Then asked, "You can't get here after detention?"

Fortunately, Devon had thought this through. "No. I miss the school bus so I have to take the public bus. I won't get home till late."

"No worries, man. We'll cover you for next week. Now, get outa here."

Devon was never so glad to head home.

When Devon was out of sight, Biggie opened the bundle of money, distributing some of it among the boys, then pocketing the rest.

"Well, gentleman. It looks like we got ourselves another line of business."

One of the boys, Jeremiah, nervously stuffed the money in his pocket. "We gotta be careful, Biggie. If the Jaguar finds out, he won't be happy.'"

“You let me do the worrin', Bad Boy. Besides, if the Jag wanted us to do more o' his business, he'd 'a given it to us. It's not like I haven't been askin'.”

“Yeah, man.” One of the other boys gave him a shove. “Stop looking for trouble.”

“Okay, boys,” Biggie stepped in. “Let's break for the night. Tomorrow, same time.”

The boys all agreed and went their separate ways. Biggie hung around the corner for a moment, counting his money.

Across the street, in a second-floor apartment, two undercover cops watched the exchange.

Chapter 23

#999

Vince hadn't been by much since Lanie's death, something he wasn't proud of. As they sat at Leo's kitchen table, he noticed the house had an eerie emptiness to it, like if you listened close enough, you could hear echoes of laughter and conversations. He didn't know how Leo did it. It must break his heart anew every morning. He wasn't at all sure how he'd hold up if anything happened to Carla. If Leo was going a little off the deep end, he could understand it.

"So, why don't you start by telling me what exactly happened in Nepal?" Vince folded his hands in front of him on the table.

Leo proceeded to tell Vince the whole story of the monk, the hash marks, and the legend.

"So, what's with the medallion?"

Leo reached into his shirt and produced the charm collection, holding the Buddha between his thumb and forefinger, leaving the others dangling from the chain.

"It doesn't look like much," Vince remarked.

"Heh, that's what I said. The monk assured me it was the real deal. He said he believed it would activate within a hundred feet or so of the child."

"Sweet. So, now, we just have eight hundred babies to hunt down and stand near."

"Four hundred, assuming half are girls," he shrugged. "Look, I know it sounds ridiculous."

"Ridiculous? This went past ridiculous three hundred ninety-nine babies ago."

"I know that!" Leo was getting frustrated. "Can we shift from problem finding to problem solving, please?"

"Sorry. It's just that it all seems impossible."

Leo eased up. "Let's start thinking about what we have. Like birth certificates."

"Do you really have four hundred birth certificates???"

"Of course not. I'm not that crazy. But I did print out forty or so to see what we're dealing with, hoping to narrow the search parameters a bit." He handed the pile to Vince who sifted through them, scanning each one briefly.

"So, I noticed there were things we could rule out, like some of them are not US citizens or have home addresses other than New York City. They are probably home already. It doesn't mean that they aren't the Buddha, just that it's difficult to track them."

"Yeah, I'm noticing that. Even in just this small sample, there's a few."

"It's a growing tourist business."

"What is?" Vince looked up from the papers.

"Foreign nationals having babies in the US. Women come here for the last few weeks of their pregnancy and give birth, resulting in a baby that has dual citizenship. Then they go home and when the child is eighteen, they declare US citizenship, come here and send for their families."

"You're kidding."

"Nope. It's long-range immigration planning. And it's nearly foolproof. All you need is money to get here, upwards of $20,000 US dollars and then 18 years to wait. It's more than that, though. It's a promise to their children for something better."

"Wow. That's a powerful picture of what US citizenship means to the world. Where are they coming from?"

"In New York, it's mostly Eastern Europe. LA is the destination for Chinese expectant mothers."

"Well, you've certainly done your homework on this."

"Yeah, lots of time on my hands, I suppose." Leo shrugged and shook his head. "Anyway, for now we might be able to eliminate some of the births that way and others by different filters on the search. We can filter by boroughs, and other things, until we have a starting point."

"Clearly, you've thought about this a lot."

"I have."

"You're starting to look less crazy." Vince nodded his head in approval.

"Thanks."

"So, what happens when you have a starting point?"

"Taking the hundred-foot radius into account, I figure a drive-by or standing on the sidewalk will get us close enough for a lot of places. Brownstones and townhouses come right up to the sidewalk. For apartment buildings, maybe we have to go floor to floor if we can get in. I just figure we'll wing it."

"I keep hearing we. You're not thinking I'm a ride-along on this, are you? I still have a job, you know."

“Relax, Vince. You’re off that hook. But some locker-room support would be nice.”

“I can cover that. Starting when?”

“Well, I can start as soon as we chunk things down. Which brings me around to a different question. What have you told Carla?”

“Nothing yet. But she knows something is up. I told her I'd have more to say when I got back from here. And I'm not lying to her or keeping secrets.”

“I get it. I’m not asking you to. You know, I can go talk to her myself. After all, I've known her longer than you have.” It was a standard rib between them. Technically, Leo had spotted Carla first at the bar the night they all met. And it was Leo who made the first pass at talking to her. That was twenty-five years ago. The comment was enough to take the edge off.

“But I know her better,” he grinned. “I think I should play this one first, in case it gets ugly.” They both knew Carla had a passion about things.

Leo walked him to the door. It felt good to have Vince onboard. They exchanged a slap-on-the-back guy hug.

“We'll figure this out, man,”

“Yeah, thanks, Vince. It means a lot knowing you're with me on this,” Leo said as his friend headed out the door. “Let me know what Carla has to say...but only if it's good,” Leo called after him.

Chapter 24

#998

Fr. Rico Santori was in his office in Rome preparing his Sunday sermon when there was a knock at the door. It was a Fed Ex driver with the delivery of an overnight envelope.

"Sign here," the man instructed, handing him a clipboard.

"Yes, certainly. I hardly ever get packages," he joked. "It must be a special day."

"Yes, sir, Father. I'm sure it is," The man quickly took back the clipboard and hustled out the door.

"Have a nice day," Father Rico called after him. "Hm, what do we have here?" he mumbled on his way back to his office. Using the pull-tab, he drew the red tape across the top, opened the cardboard jacket and tipped the contents out onto a small table just inside his office.

He sucked his breath in when he saw the letter. It was on handmade paper and sealed with the wax impression of the Buddha. He knew the seal. It belonged to the commander of The Knowledge Keepers. What could he possibly be sending him? Hands slightly trembling, he broke the seal.

Father Rico,

Your services are needed immediately at the Church of Saint Barbara, Dededo, Guam. A male child, #998, has been identified as needing our support. I assume you will have no problem getting assigned there. Update me of your progress.

Brother Li Chin

Father Rico read the message three times. It was short and to the point. There was no gray area. He had secretly hoped he would be called someday, but he never really believe it would happen. Certainly not after all these years. Now, here it was, a summons to prepare the next Buddha, to prepare humanity for what comes next. The Christian scripture calls it the Second Coming. Islam also teaches that a second coming of Christ will herald a new era. The Jews are awaiting the first Messiah. Rastafari and Baha'i traditions believe that Christ has already come again. The Hindus believed in many gods and saints, even present-day holy men who perform miracles. Father Rico always wondered if maybe those manifestations were some of the Thousand. Secretly, his favorite prophecy, put forth by Paramahansa Yogananda, was that the next coming of the Christ would be in the hearts of every human being. Yogananda cites Luke 17:21, "Neither shall they say, lo here! or, lo there! for, behold, the kingdom of God is within you." Imagine if God lit up the hearts of every man, woman, and child on earth with the love and compassion of the Holy Spirit. What a great day that would be.

The letter had taken the wind out of him. Although a not-so-old 64, age had started to claim its birthright. Small aches and pains mostly, and his blood pressure had not been good in recent years. Out of breath, he leaned on various pieces of furniture on his way back to his desk and finally to his chair where he sat staring into space and recalling a day thirty-odd years ago.

Father Rico had received a request, handwritten, from Pope John Paul I for a meeting, with instructions that he was to tell no one. When he arrived at the Pope's chambers, all the assistants had been dismissed for the day. The meeting lasted for two hours where Pope John Paul I described the relationship between the Church and The Knowledge Keepers, beginning with Pope Clement IX in 1668. He remembered it as if it was yesterday.

"A monk named Gathnadi approached the pope with a fascinating tale of the 1000th Buddha who would take humanity into the next age but only if a certain number survived. At the time, these Buddhas were dying at the hands of the catholic church, accused of heresy and executed all over Europe." John Paul paused to shake his head at the thought. "A few broad-thinking holy people around the world drafted agreements to cooperate in any way necessary to foster the well-being of the next Buddha."

"Excuse me, Your Excellence, but why are we concerned with heathen fairy tales?" Fr. Rico asked.

The Pope gave him a stern look that silenced him.

"Because," the pontiff went on, "from our perspective it sounded a lot like the Second Coming of Christ and we didn't want to be responsible for executing him—or her." The pope paused until he saw understanding dawn on Fr. Rico's face. "Clement began quietly to discourage accusations and executions, without much result. The politico-religious fervor sadly continued for hundreds of years after that." Pope John Paul shook his head again. "Clement's collaboration with other faiths was discovered by the inner sanctum and taken as heresy. He died mysteriously a few months later."

Pope John Paul I instructed Father Rico to get himself reassigned to a church in Nepal where he would be educated on the esoteric teachings long-ago banned from Christianity. He should tell no one about their conversation. Two days later, Pope John Paul I was found dead in his chambers from unknown causes, or so went the official story from the Vatican, after just 32 days in office. Father Rico never spoke about it again, to anyone, save the other members of The Knowledge Keepers.

It seemed a lifetime ago and although he had kept in touch with the order, his belief in the mission had waned, almost to disbelief. Now, heart pumping in his chest, he tried desperately to recall the teachings that had drifted into the back of his consciousness.

The most immediate action was to get the transfer papers submitted. He had a good friend at the assignments office but he'd still need a good reason for a speedy transfer, and to Guam of all places. Maybe his friend wouldn't ask.

Chapter 25

#998

Sarah had been out of sorts since her strange encounter with Brother Bensi. What was she supposed to do now? The monk in the cave had not been very specific about what to do next. She was feeling more than a little irritated by the whole thing when Fr. Rico arrived. Thankfully, the Riveras had pushed the baptism off until after the holidays.

Sarah answered the knock at the door.

"Hello. I'm Father Rico Santori. I'm here to meet with Mrs. Rivera." He waited politely to be invited in.

Sarah looked him up and down suspiciously. She had become a little overcautious where James was concerned. After all, she was responsible for his safety. What if the Catholic Church screwed him up somehow, preventing him from his destiny? She didn't like this situation one bit.

"Yes, come in." She tried for casual indifference. "Marion is just bringing James downstairs. He was sleeping," she added accusingly.

"She really didn't have to wake him for me. And you are?" he asked pleasantly.

"Sarah Sullivan. I'm James' nanny."

"Sarah?" Fr. Rico was caught off guard. The commander had alerted him to a woman named Sarah who was enlisted to locate the child, but he didn't expect her to be in the house with James. He wasn't sure if he should be concerned or not.

She was a little disturbed by his response, like he knew her name somehow. "Yes. Has Marion told you about me?"

"No." Father Rico's voice was almost a whisper. "Word came to me from Nepal."

Sarah was stunned and super cautious. "What do you mean?"

He noticed a chain around her neck. "I believe we are on the same mission." He pulled a watch chain out of his pocket. At the end of the chain, laying against the back of the time piece, was a medallion similar to hers.

She looked at him, confused, memories of Brother Bensi and the monk in the cave collided in her head. She opened her mouth to speak but nothing came out.

"I'm sorry to startle you," he was still whispering. "I just wanted you to know that I am on your team. We can talk more at a later date."

Just then, Marion came down the stairs cradling a sleeping baby.

"Hello Fr. Rico. Thank you for coming."

Fr. Rico instantly shifted his attention and demeanor. "Hello Mrs. Rivera," he nodded to her.

"Please, call me Marion," she replied, "and this is James

Lee." She presented the baby to Fr. Rico as if for inspection.

Fr. Rico cooed appropriately, admiring the infant. "He's absolutely miraculous."

"Yes. He is. It looks like you've met Sarah?"

"Yes. We just introduced ourselves."

She turned to look at Sarah. "What's wrong? You look pale."

"Nothing," Sarah almost stammered. "I'll just finish cleaning up and head home. I'll see you tomorrow."

"Yes, of course, Sarah. Thank you."

Sarah nodded to Fr. Rico before she darted out of the room.

Meanwhile, Brother Bensi was sitting in the sweltering heat in a small village south of Shanghai wondering what he did that had caused this unfortunate turn of events. He played over the conversation with the young girl in Guam. What was her name? Yes, Sarah. Next thing he knew, he was here, in the middle of nowhere, with indoor plumbing as the most recent modern convenience.

Was there something to her story? If so, the powers that be had treated him rather shabbily. They obviously didn't hold him to be of any importance. Well, maybe someone else would. After all, it was an interesting piece of information he had come by. Surely it would be of value to the right person. The days went by painfully slowly here and he had a lot of time to think about it.

Chapter 26

#997

The days passed swiftly for Nathan and Kate. Between their usual double holiday Chanukah/Christmas and their wedding on New Year's Eve, life had been non-stop. Kate's belly continued to swell and attention shifted as soon as the holidays were over. Kate was becoming increasingly anxious about being ready for their due date of March 1st. Nursery furniture, assembly required, was being delivered tomorrow, and they were starting birthing classes next week. Nathan was doing his best to keep her calm.

"I don't know, Nate. I have a bad feeling, not that something's wrong, but that things aren't going to go the way their supposed to."

"I'm sure it will be fine, honey. The doctors all gave you a five-star bill of health."

"I know that. I'm just saying…let's be as ready as we can."

In Kate's usual fashion, she had a notebook of all things

baby that started with a monthly calendar and included tabs for furniture, baby items like clothing, diapers, etc., a family support schedule and all possible scenarios when labor started. She had planned out a total of ten routes to the hospital, depending on where they were coming from and likely traffic at various times of the day. A go bag by the door was quickly accumulating necessary items for the hospital.

Nathan tried to split his attention between Kate and Devon, not always successfully, and he knew Kate worried that his priorities were not where she'd like them to be. Fortunately, Devon's situation seemed to be stable as far as he could tell. Basketball season was progressing and Nathan never missed a game. Brother Chen had stepped in as well, to help keep an eye on the boy Buddha, relieving some of Nathan's stress.

"Devon wants to keep some of his Christmas gifts at the temple," Nathan said, hoping to calm some of her nerves.

"He doesn't want to bring new things home. Either they will get taken away, or he'll get in trouble for asking for handouts."

"Really, Kate. Do you always have to be a naysayer?" Nathan had criticized.

"Say what you like. The boy's in trouble."

Although not technically a Buddhist holiday, the Temple celebrated a modified Christmas for its members, invoking prayers for a peaceful world.

"Wow, Devon. That's quite a lot of gifts." Brother Chen indicated the pile of clothing and electronics. "The staff here really like you and appreciate you."

"Yeah. I don't know what to say. It's a lot of stuff."

Devon was kicking the air and looking downward.

"What's the problem?" Chen asked.

"Well, I'm thinking maybe I could keep it here, instead of bringing it home. You know, so I'll have some stuff here when I need it."

Chen was a little suspicious but took it as an opportunity to keep the boy close by. "Sure. No problem. We can set you up with some space in the closet in the office area. How would that be?"

"Great. Thanks."

Devon had shown up to Biggie and the crew one time in new sneakers. They abruptly confiscated them, then Biggie warned him about "gettin' wit' anyone outside the 'hood'. We take care o' you now."

And so, Devon was left balancing both worlds while trying to escape the fate of the neighborhood.

Chapter 27

#999

Sifting through eight hundred birth records had proved tedious and time consuming. Even with the electronic search methods available, Leo was left with three hundred seventy-seven female babies remaining in New York City. With Vince's help, they grouped them together by boroughs, then by blocks, then by streets. It took hours to plot them on a wall-sized map in Leo's kitchen. Then, they isolated a list for Brooklyn, Leo's area.

"Can I just say, Holy Shit, Lee." Vince was gazing at the final product.

"Yeah," Leo stared at the map. "Somewhere along the way I realized that this could be a very long project. Even if I drive by all these addresses, there's no guarantee that the baby is there. And we'll run out of the twelve-week maternity leave soon enough, so, even if they're home now, they might not be in another month or two."

"It's starting to feel like a fool's errand, Lee. You don't even know what you're going to do if you find this baby."

"I'm trying not to get discouraged."

"Are you sure this monk was for real?"

"Really, Vince? Let's not go over that again."

Vince ran his fingers through his hair. "Okay. Sorry. I couldn't help myself."

"I've been beating my brains out trying to come up with a better plan, and can't. You?"

"Nope."

"So, this is what we got."

He had become obsessed with his search. Vince, noticing his intensity, had cautioned him about burning out before the task was complete. So, he'd limited himself to four hours a day, not including travel time to the search location. He got into the habit of eating lunch at the closest park, checking out the children in the playground. He felt a little creepy doing it and occasionally got ugly stares from mothers, but he didn't want to pass up a random encounter.

It was an unusually warm January day, when Leo headed out for his daily baby walk, as he was calling it. Each day, he isolated a section of the city, drove there, then got out and walked the streets indicated as having babies born on December 13th. He went out every day, no matter the weather, so he was grateful for today's sun. A warm southerly wind had driven the temps to the high fifties, coaxing New Yorkers out of their winter hibernations, even if only for a day or two. The tradeoff was slush-filled streets and muddy playgrounds.

He'd been searching for four weeks already, making the rounds through each borough then starting again. Today, he was back in his home borough of Brooklyn, where he determined one hundred thirty-six potential Baby 13s, a nickname Vince had given them, were living. Surprisingly there were three just on his own block. Wouldn't that be nice if the baby showed up so conveniently. But he had no luck close to home and his search had expanded out from there. His radar for babies had disappeared over the years. When he was a parent, he saw them everywhere. Now, with his daughter, twenty-two and living in Los Angeles, he barely noticed. Add to that, his depression over the past few months and he had become oblivious to the world around him.

Today, he passed by fourteen addresses on his morning walk through a densely populated neighborhood in Brooklyn. There were a couple of apartment buildings he couldn't get into, so he decided to break for lunch and try again later, before he quit for the day. He stopped to pick up a sandwich at the local market, then headed over to a park he'd passed earlier.

As he turned the corner to the park, he saw a woman sitting on a bench alone with a small baby in her lap. The baby was wailing loudly. The mom was barely holding onto the child as she sobbed uncontrollably. Leo forgot all about his quest at that moment, and headed quickly to the woman to offer her support and assistance.

He slowed down as he approached her. He didn't want to alarm her.

"Hi. Ah, are you alright?"

The women's sobs lightened as she tried to gain some composure. "Leave me alone," she whimpered.

"Look, I just want to help."

"Go away," she said without much conviction.

“I notice your baby is crying. It sounds like colic to me.”

That got her attention. “She won't stop crying. I don't know what to do. I'm shit for a mother.”

Leo had inched his way toward her. He was nervous. He didn't want this woman to suddenly start screaming for the police or something. “I had a colicky baby, too. Maybe I can help.” He tentatively reached out his arms to take the baby.

She winced and turned away slightly, pulling the baby closer to her.

“Really. I'm one of the good guys. I just want to help. I'm going to sit right here, next to you.” Leo gestured to the far end of the park bench. “Alright?”

She made no reply.

“Okay, I'm sitting down right here.” He set himself down, placing his lunch on the ground in front of him. He could feel his adrenaline pumping and was trying to calm himself down. “I know what you're going through. Honestly. My daughter had me in tears many times. I thought for sure I was screwing her up for life before she could even walk.”

The woman turned slightly back toward him.

“My wife was a great help. Do you have anyone?”

“He's dead,” she replied flatly, the baby still screaming in her lap.

Leo's heart broke a little for both their losses. “My wife's dead, too.” He choked a little on the words.

For the first time, she made significant eye contact, as if to challenge his statement.

“It's true,” he nodded. “This past October, in a car accident.” He paused before going on. “And I really did have a colicky baby. I developed my own little tricks to calm her down. Can I give them a try for your little girl?”

The woman looked at him for a long moment, then

nodded slightly.

"Is she hungry?" Leo asked as he reached over and gently took the small being in his hands.

"I just fed her a few minutes ago. That's when she started screaming."

She was tiny. He turned her over on her stomach and rested her on his arm. He patted her back three times, then rubbed in a circle three times, then waited. He kept repeating the routine and, within a minute, the infant had settled down.

The woman looked at him in awe, then started sobbing again. "I suck at this. I have no business having a baby. My husband wanted her more than I did. What does that say about me?"

"It says that you loved your husband," Leo replied as he gently rocked the baby.

"I did," she sobbed. "He was everything to me. We were going to do this together."

He slid toward her, close enough to offer her a sideways hug while securing the baby in his other arm. She accepted the hug, cautiously at first but then gave into his embrace, quieting herself down again.

He could really feel his adrenaline now, and a pulsing in his chest. He took a deep breath, trying to calm his own nerves. The pulsing started to become a vibration. He suddenly realized that what he thought was nerves and adrenaline, was really the medallion, going crazy under his shirt. He could barely breath. He knew it was critical to remain calm, and not spook this fragile mother. With all the self-control he could muster, he said, "I have some lunch. We can share. I'm sure you haven't eaten in a while."

She didn't respond.

"Why don't we go sit at the picnic table over there and

talk and eat while little...?" He fished for the baby's name.

"Ellie."

"Ellie," he repeated. "It's a beautiful name. While little Ellie sleeps it off. What do you say? I'll grab the lunch and you push the stroller."

"I'm not even sure I can stand." She shook her head and started to cry again.

"That's okay. Look, I'm putting Ellie back in the stroller and I can help you."

She nodded her head. "Okay," she said weakly.

Leo gently secured the baby in the stroller, turned it in the direction of the nearest picnic table, then offered the woman his arm. She looked frail, almost lifeless.

"Hey, I don't even know your name."

"Jordan."

"Well, Jordan, my name's Leo. Let's go have lunch."

She took his arm and, with an unsteady gait, made her way to the table. Once they were sitting down, Leo took stock of the situation. Jordan appeared to be in her mid-thirties, well-dressed if somewhat unkempt. The stroller wasn't the most expensive model but it wasn't the cheapest either. Aside from a few spare diapers and blankets, it was empty. No purse. No personal items that he could see. She must live close by.

Ellie continued to sleep, probably exhausted from the morning's ordeal. He knew she wouldn't sleep for long though, once the hunger pains set in again.

"Here," he said as he unwrapped his sandwich. "I hope you like corn beef on rye."

"What New Yorker doesn't like corn beef on rye?" she mumbled.

"Hey," he smiled at her. "Was that a joke?"

"I guess so," she smiled back, taking half of the overstuffed meat-eaters delight. "Mustard or mayo?"

"Both."

"Good choice."

"What did your husband do?" Leo asked just before he loaded his mouth with corn beef, and trying to ignore the sensation on his chest.

"NYPD Narcotics. Killed in a raid on a meth lab." Jordan sampled her half of the sandwich timidly, then went in for real bite. She was amazed at how hungry she was.

"Tough call."

"Aren't you going to say 'thank you for his service' or 'he was an honorable man' or 'he died a hero' or some other platitude?"

"Nope. Remember, I've heard it all, too. Six months ago. 'She was such good person.' 'So young. What a tragedy.' 'At least you have your daughter.' That's the one that always got under my skin. Like she's the consolation prize or they're interchangeable."

"Yeah. Mine was 'you should be proud of him'. Like I need your permission, first of all. And, oh yeah," she leaned over the table at him, "he's freaking dead!" she said angrily. Then backed off. "Oh, sorry." She settled back down.

"Don't be. I get it. How long has it been?"

"Four months. Two months later, to the day, Ellie was born. I haven't been able to pull it together." She looked away, shaking her head.

"My job gave me a generous three months off and I still couldn't pull together. Finally, they said come back to work or resign, so, I quit. I got a little bit of life insurance money and they'll be an insurance settlement down the road, so I can hang out for a little while anyway. But it's not much and it doesn't make me feel any better."

"I know. People think that when you die on the job, there's this big financial windfall, but there isn't and I don't know what I'm going to do when the money runs out."

"Don't you have anyone to help you? Family? Friends?"

"Sure. They were all over the place for the first few weeks, then they scattered, got back to their lives, said 'call if you need anything'."

"Yeah. I know that, too. My friends avoid talking about my wife, afraid they'll upset me. But, you know, not talking about her upsets me. I want to remember her. I want to talk about her. She existed!"

"Yeah. Conversations were always strained just before they stopped showing up."

Leo thought he saw some color coming back into her face. "How are you feeling, now?" he asked as he collected the empty sandwich wrappers and chips bag.

"Better. Thank you. I can truly say, I don't know what I would have done. I was at my wits end."

"I should thank you. It's every man's secret fantasy to save a damsel in distress." He flashed her a smile.

"Well, you can check off that box." When she smiled back, he caught a tiny twinkle in her eyes.

"Thank you, madame." He placed a hand on his chest and the other out to the side in a gallant bow. "Let me top it off by seeing you safely home."

She hesitated a moment. "I don't know. I think I'm fine."

"Excuse me, but I don't think you are. And I can't check off the box if I don't see it through till the end."

"Okay," she relented. She knew he was right. She was still pretty shaky and, truthfully, she didn't want to be alone. "I just live around the corner."

"Great." Leo went around the table to help her up. She didn't really need the help but she appreciated the human contact. So did he.

"Let me get that," he offered as she reached for the stroller.

"No. It's alright. I'll use it to lean on."

"Good enough."

Together they headed out of the park at a slow pace. Jordan, because she couldn't go any faster. Leo, because he was stalling for time, trying to think of a way to stay connected to this family.

He walked along beside her with his hands in his pockets. "You know, Jordan. I'm not working right now and I've got plenty of time on my hands. I'd really like to be helpful to you and Ellie."

She didn't say anything.

"Not a big deal. Just checking in on you, picking up diapers and groceries, whatever you need. Your guy Friday. What do you say?"

"I don't know."

"Okay. Think about it."

They walked in silence until Jordan slowed down in front of a concrete staircase leading to the glass door of an apartment building. The address was 235 Oakhurst Street. He was sure it was on his list for this afternoon.

"Thanks again, Leo." Jordan turned around, positioning herself to go backwards up the stairs pulling the stroller.

"Oh, no. Let me help you with that." He shooed her out of the way, carefully picked up the stroller and baby and walked it up the stairs, one step at a time. Fortunately, Ellie was still out like a light. "What floor are you on?"

She didn't have the energy to argue and she wasn't sure

she wanted to. “This is my place right here.” She pointed to the windows on the first floor to the left. “I have to warn you, the place is a little messy.”

“No problem. I know what it's like to have a newborn. I'd be surprised if it was any other way.” He followed her into the front hallway. It was a clean entryway, in good repair, indicating either condos or a conscientious landlord.

“Come on in,” she said halfheartedly as she unlocked the door. He allowed her to enter the apartment, politely giving her some space, then followed in behind her.

Like the foyer, it was in good condition, tastefully decorated with quality furniture. And it was more than just messy. It was a wreck. Half-eaten dinners lined up on the dining room table. Nearly empty casserole dishes were stacked on the kitchen pass-through counter, no doubt the remains of food brought by well-intended friends and family. Take out containers littered the coffee table. Burp cloths and blankets everywhere. At least dirty diapers had made it to the trash.

“Just as I suspected,” Leo tried to joke, “the home of a new parent. I recognize it right away.”

“You're too kind. I know it's a train wreck.” She made a halfhearted effort to straighten up.

“Look, one of the rules my wife and I had early on was that when the baby slept, she slept. I know you can't always do that, but you can right now. Why don't you go lay down with Ellie and I'll straighten up a little before I go?”

Again, she hesitated. She needed the help. She knew that. But logic told her not to trust this guy she'd just met in the park an hour ago.

Noting her caution, he added quickly, “Or I can go. Really. No pressure.”

She pushed logic aside and went with intuition. "I can't tell you how much I appreciate this. You have no idea."

"My pleasure. I'd just be sitting home alone anyway, worrying about how you're doing. Let me get you settled." He carried Ellie into the bedroom where he spotted a bassinet next to the bed. Gently, he placed Ellie on her back and was tucking her in when Jordan shooed him out.

"I've got it, but thank you."

"No problem." Leo closed the bedroom door on his way out.

As he straightened up the apartment, he began to formulate a plan. He would come by daily to help out for now. As time went on, maybe he could mentor the girl-without-a-dad. The monk had never said what to do once he found the girl and he never thought to ask. It was unbelievable that he found her at all and, according to the Mezuzah on the door jam, she was Jewish.

Chapter 28

#997

For Devon, the holidays went by pretty much the same as all the other days. He was grateful for the generosity of the Buddhist, but he knew all good things come to an end sooner or later. He was just biding his time until the next disappointment.

After the fabricated week of detention, Devon had to come up with another excuse to keep him away from Biggie and the boys as much as he could. He asked Brother Chen if he could just work three days at first. Brother Chen easily agreed. He liked the monk. He didn't know anything about Buddhism, but at least the guy in charge was nice. And a hot meal every night! He really couldn't turn it down. So, he concocted a story for Biggie that he hoped would ease him out of their grip. He would claim he had been referred to an after-school program for problem kids. It was mandatory, three afternoons a week. Biggie wouldn't like it, but he'd already figured out a replacement so maybe he could slip out.

Today was one of the days he ran money. He didn't like making the second stop. It always smelled like harsh chemicals. He knew it would mean trouble sooner or later. But it was none of his business, and he planned to keep it that way.

Biggie seemed a little jumpy today.

"You goin' to the second stop today, right? Same as usual." It wasn't really a question, more a confirmation.

"Yeah, Biggie. Just like usual."

"Get in and get out fast. Make sure nobody sees you. Right?"

"Yeah. I got it. Something going down?" Devon was getting worried.

"Nothing I know of. Just being cautious."

The other boys were strangely quiet today, standing off to the side.

"Are you sure?"

"Yeah! I'm sure!" Biggie was irritated. "Just do it."

"Okay."

While Devon was making the first stop, law enforcement officers were placing themselves strategically around the second house. They'd been watching the property for several weeks. In addition to the meth lab, they were trafficking women and children from Central America. The FBI was part of the team setting up to raid the place this afternoon. They were all hooked up through ear buds, just like on TV.

"What do you see, Alpha?"

"Nothing on the outside. Clear down the block."

"Bravo? What do you have?"

"Two adolescent females I can see from the window. I can't see the two men that entered earlier."

"Charlie?"

"Two pedestrians on the street. They don't look to be part of this. I think they'll be gone in a minute or two."

"Alright. As soon as they're clear, we go." Captain Albreight, of NYPD was commanding the joint task force. Six officers all together. The FBI had let the local authorities take lead and there was a lot riding on this for him. If it went well, it meant at least a promotion and maybe a job offer from the Feds, and with the added bonus of getting these dirt bags off the street, of course.

A moment later, Charlie gave the all clear over the airwaves.

"That's it, people. Go! Go!" Albreight gave the command.

"Hold up, Captain! I got a kid going in through the back door." It was Alpha calling out.

"To late! Go! Go! Go!" he yelled in the earpieces.

Five officers swarmed the house, bashing in the doors on both sides. The men inside immediately started firing their weapons. Smoke bombs went off. Chaos erupted. Flashes from the gunfire lit up the smoke. Women screamed. Devon got pushed into the fray, disoriented, blinded by the smoke. He felt a sharp pain in his chest, then difficulty breathing. Warn liquid began soaking his shirt. He heard someone shout, "Watch out for the kid!" just before he hit the floor.

He put a hand to his chest. It was warm and wet. He still couldn't see anything, but the gunfire had stopped. Men were screaming orders. Someone busted out windows to let the smoke out. He heard radios mumbling in staticky voices, something about an ambulance.

"Oh, shit. It's the kid," someone was saying.

A shadow leaned over him.

"Can you hear me, kid? Kid?" the shadow yelled.

Devon could hear him, but he couldn't move, couldn't respond, couldn't say I'm sorry. I tried to get out but I couldn't.

"Hang on kid!" He felt pressure on his chest, a rhythmic thumping. He tried to talk. Tell Brother Chen I'm sorry. I know he tried. The 'hood just doesn't let you go. No matter what. It's just like that.

Suddenly, the thumping stopped and an electric current rammed its way through his body. He felt himself lift off the ground. Then again. He knew it was no use. He appreciated that people were trying though. He knew his mom would appreciate it. He heard a voice calling his name. It was time to go.

Everyone in the room was standing still, holding their breath, watching, waiting. The EMT sat back on his heels. He wiped sweat from his face, or was it tears. "Time of death 17:53."

In a quiet cave, deep in the Himalayas, a solitary monk was aroused out of his meditation. Slowly, he stood, walked to the opposite wall, and with a piece of charcoal, placed a hash mark across a line, leaving two marks remaining uncrossed. He bowed his head in silent prayer before returning to his meditation.

Chapter 29

#997

Nathan's phone rang late that evening. It was the principal at Rosa Parks Middle School.

"Nathan, it's Doc Lasser here. I'm sorry to bother you."

"No problem. What can I do for you?" Nathan was expecting a change in scheduling for something or a last-minute request. He knew teachers and administrators worked long hours making things run smoothly all day.

"I have some news for you. I didn't want you to see it on TV first."

"Oh? Okay." Although it sounded serious, Nathan was expecting some administrative budget cutting or other political shenanigans.

"There's been a shooting. A house raid in the Beaumont neighborhood."

"What! When?" His mind was racing, his heart pounding.

"This afternoon."

"Devon!" he yelled into the phone.

"I'm afraid so. Caught in the crossfire is what I understand at this moment. I don't have any details." Doc Lasser paused to let the information sink in. "He was pronounced dead at the scene. They found his school ID and called me for contact info. There's an officer headed over to his house now."

Nathan was silent.

"I know you were close with him, right? Trying to keep him out of harm's way? I thought you might want to hear it from me."

Nathan couldn't breathe.

Kate came running into the room when she heard him shout Devon's name. She saw him, frozen, holding the phone.

"What's going on!" She grabbed the phone from him. "What happened?" she demanded into the phone.

Nathan got his wits about him and took the phone back. He said, "Thank you, Doc," and hung up.

Kate was near panic. "What happened?"

"There was a shooting in Beaumont."

"Oh, no."

"Devon was killed in the crossfire."

"No. No. It can't be." Kate grabbed her belly and stumbled backward. Nathan rushed to her side and helped her to the couch where they both sat in stunned silence.

"Are you sure?" Kate could barely speak.

"They're notifying his mother right now."

"Dear God. What happened?"

Nathan relayed what little information he had.

"Should we call Brother Chen?"

"No. It's late. I'll call first thing in the morning."

Kate and Nathan decided to go to the temple personally,

arriving for morning services. They took the opportunity to sit for meditation with the community before seeking out Brother Chen. Many of the monks knew Devon by now, seeing him after school working around the facilities. None knew the full truth of it, as far as they knew.

When they asked about the senior monk, they were directed to the back office. Nathan was trying to decide how to start the conversation as they made their way through the hallways. He'd run it over in his head a hundred times already, realizing there's no good way to say it. Still, he thought a slow lead-in would help ease the blow.

"Good morning Brother Chen," Nathan greeted him as he entered the office.

Immediately, the monk was on his feet. "Is it Devon? What has happened?"

The direct question threw Nathan off his game. Kate stepped in. "I'm afraid there's been an accident, well, not really an accident exactly."

"I saw the shooting in Beaumont on the news last night. Please tell me the boy is safe."

There was a long pause.

The monk collapsed back into his chair. "I knew it. I felt it. Tell me."

Nathan found his voice. "There was a shooting as you know. Apparently, Devon was caught in the middle somehow. We don't know what he was doing there, not that it matters now."

The monk bowed his head and shook it from side to side. "The loss is immeasurable. You have no idea."

"With all due respect, Brother, I think we do," Kate replied.

Brother Chen looked up to see tears running down Kate's

cheeks. “Yes. My apologies. I'm sure you do.”

Kate and Nathan had fully invested themselves into this mission, hook, line and sinker. Their studies of the Buddhist tradition gave them a deep understanding of the importance of their task which they took very seriously. The memory of the cave came vividly into Nathan's mind. In that moment, the enormity of his failure came suddenly into focus. Not only had a young boy died on his watch – a boy they had come to love and respect, but a holy being didn’t get to live out a miraculous life and the entire human race was now in peril. He slumped over in his chair.

“This is unreal. How could this happen?” He stifled the sob in his throat, then anger took over his grief. “I got cocky. That's what happened, prideful, thinking this was going to be easy.” Nathan pounded his fist into his leg. “I should have paid more attention. I should have seen this coming. The monk will know I have failed him.” The thought of disappointing the monk in the cave was the final blow. He leaned forward, resting his elbows on his knees, head in his hands, and began to sob. Kate, rubbing his back, joined him in his grief.

“Hundreds of Buddhas have been unsuccessful at their task. We cannot assume responsibility here,” Brother Chen added gently. “There are many powers at play. Failure is built into the process.” He paused, then continued, “Nonetheless, I, too, feel a sense of responsibility. For my entire life, I have been training for this one purpose. Failure to remove the boy from danger will certainly haunt me.”

“What happens now?” Nathan almost pleaded. “Is mankind doomed?”

“There are still others who have the opportunity to fulfill the legend if mankind is worthy.”

"How many others?" Kate was asking. "Are they children? Can we help?"

"Two others have taken physical form. One yet to manifest. I have no other details."

"Maybe I can go back to the cave, talk to the monk, get another mission?" Nathan was desperate to make this right.

"Your obligation has passed. There are others working on theirs. Our task now is to pray."

Chapter 30

#999

"You did what?" Carla was winding up to read him the riot act. "Are you crazy? She might call the police, have you arrested! What's wrong with you, going into her house!"

"Calm down, sweetie," Vince tried to intervene. "Can you please let the man speak?"

"Well, he'd better talk fast."

"Listen, Carla," Leo started, "It's not what you think. I just went up to a woman in the park who was clearly having a hard time. That's all. And next thing I know, this thing around my neck is practically jumping out of my shirt. What did you want me to do? Leave her there crying with a newborn baby?"

"She was crying?" Carla's attitude shifted.

"Yes. It was not a good scene. I was just being a good guy, and she needed it. She was a mess."

"Alright," she yielded slightly before demanding, "Tell me everything."

Leo filled Vince and Carla in on the events in the park

and then at Jordan's house. "She was still sleeping when I left, so I wrote a note, leaving my name and phone number, and telling her I'd be back tomorrow morning." He looked at Carla. "Do you really think she'll call the cops? She probably knows a lot of them."

"Who knows," Carla shrugged. "If she has postpartum depression, hard saying what she'll do."

"Oh, no. Do you think the baby is okay?" Panic gripped Leo around the chest.

"Look," Vince's voice came calmly into focus. "I'm sure she'll be fine 'til tomorrow when you can check things out again and see what she needs."

"Yeah. You're right. No sense blowing things out of proportion." But Leo couldn't shake the panic Carla's comment had fired up. Just then, his phone rang. He didn't recognize the number but he answered anyway, just in case.

"Hello?"

"Hi. Leo?" Jordan's voice came over the phone.

"Yes, Jordan. Hi. Is everything okay?"

"Yes. Yes. I just wanted to call and say thank you for today. You're a very kind man."

"It was my pleasure."

"But you really don't have to come by tomorrow. We'll be fine."

"No. No. It's no trouble and it would make me feel so much better to just check in. Quick. In and out. Just hello. And besides, I accidentally fell in love with Ellie."

"Well, that I can understand."

"Really. I'm not a stalker. In fact, I'm over at a friend's house telling them about how nice it was to be helpful. Do you want to talk to them? They'll vouch for me. Well, maybe not Vince. But Carla for sure."

"No. It's not necessary. I believe you."

"So, let me stop by in the morning. I'll bring bagels."

"With lox?"

"Any way you want 'em."

"I won't let you in without the lox."

"I'll be there. Nine-thirty?"

"Alright. Fine."

"See you then."

"And thank you, Leo." She hung up before he could say anything else.

Leo was stoked. "Yes!" he emphasized it with a fist pump. "I'm going over in the morning." He was smiling from ear to ear.

Carla picked up on it. "I think you're a little too happy about this. What does this woman look like?"

"Carla!" Vince was aghast. "What are you saying? Lanie's barely dead."

"Maybe she is, but Leo's not."

"What's wrong with you?" He turned to Leo. "I'm sorry, man. You know Carla has no filter."

"It's okay, both of you. Truth is, she's a beautiful woman. But I wasn't lying when I said I fell in love with that baby. She's the most amazing thing I've ever seen."

Chapter 31

#998

Brother Bensi had been a busy monk up in the hilltop Monastery of Divine Light. He'd managed to procure a cell phone, in direct disregard for house rules, from a shop in town. He had found a secluded spot behind the main building where he could hook into the wireless connection used by the office staff. Seeing as no one was supposed to have any electronic devices, there was no password protection and he had full use of the linkup.

He never stopped marveling at the scope of the internet. It seemed that any information you could think to ask, would be answered, as if from a divine source. So, he wasn't entirely surprised when his query into the Brotherhood of the Green Dragon netted him several options. The Green Dragon was a notoriously violent organized crime syndicate operating throughout China and Southeast Asia. Known for all manner of smuggling, they also have a history of overthrowing small governments and blackmailing political figures to their own ends. He scrolled through the selections, zeroing in on a local headline "Everything old is new again – Green Dragons return to Shanghai streets". It sounded like a divine message to him. He clicked on the article.

Green Dragon Returns – Local police officials have identified three Green Dragon members as the perpetrators of recent violence in the otherwise calm city of Shanghai. They fear a gang war for control over the human trafficking trade that has plagued the city for generations. Previously thought to be eradicated, the Green Dragon has reappeared, resulting in twelve deaths in recent weeks. The murders have been quietly and strategically executed to eliminate the top tier of the current crime operation, Sun Sin.

Brother Bensi wondered if the location of the next Buddha would be of interest to such an organization. He was willing to find out. The article had mentioned local politicians suspected of ties to the Green Dragon. Further inquiries netted office addresses for these individuals.

Creating an imaginary illness, Brother Bensi excused himself from the monastery for the day and headed to Shanghai for an alleged doctor's appointment. He wore the robes of his order, even though not technically required to for civilian activities. He found that the robes granted him a certain respect that opened doors more easily than for the average person.

This had been true this morning as he was waved through security at the office of Mr. Ti Zenghi, the Chairman of the City Council of Shanghai. His unannounced and unscheduled visit was permitted without question and he was seated in the outer office of the chairman when the door opened and Chairman Zenghi emerged to greet him.

"Welcome, Brother. I am Chairman Zenghi. How can I help you?"

"Good morning, Mr. Chairman. I am Brother Bensi and I think it is more about how I can help you."

"Already, I'm intrigued. Please come in." The chairman stepped aside to allow entrance into the office. "Have a seat, Brother Bensi, and tell me what is on your mind." Chairman Zenghi closed the door after them and took a seat at his desk.

"What would you say if I told you I have information about the location of the next Buddha?"

Zenghi tried to suppress his astonishment. "I would say that is very interesting. How is it that you come to know this, if it is, in fact, true?"

"It is quite true, I assure you. I came upon it quite by accident when a stupid girl blurted out the information, thinking I was already aware."

Zenghi considered this for a moment. "And why do you think I might be interested in this knowledge?"

"I thought it might be of value to someone with your…connections." Bensi nodded his head slightly at the reference. "I am to understand that this is the 1000th Buddha."

The chairman's eyes grew large. "That is not possible."

"That is the information I have."

"Why would you share this information with me? You obviously suspect I might take action with such knowledge?"

"The Guiding Light order I have pledged to does not appreciate my contributions and now I have been banished to a remote monastery, hours from here, due to no fault of my own. At the moment, I am simply considering my options."

"And what exactly would you be considering in exchange

for this information?"

"Safe passage out of China and enough money to live comfortably anywhere in the world."

Zenghi sat quietly for a long time, calculating both his bargaining position and what this information might do to his status in the Green Dragon. "This requires other conversations. How long do you have?"

"I must return to the monastery today. After that, the offer is off the table."

"Very well," Zenghi nodded. "Please wait at the Café Nu Zen, two blocks east of here. Someone will contact you with an answer."

"As you wish." Brother Bensi bowed as he rose from his seat. The Chairman bowed in return and Bensi left the office.

Two days later, Brother Bensi's body was loaded on a freighter and dumped at sea.

Chapter 32

#999

Leo showed up the next morning as promised, with bagels and lox. As soon as he got to the stoop, the medallion let him know he was in the presence of a saint, no matter what religion.

Jordan answered the door, already dressed and looking rested. Ellie was settled into her swing.

"How's the little angel this morning?" he asked.

"She gave me a run-around early on, but I tried that patting thing you did yesterday and it worked like a charm. How did you ever figure it out?"

"Lots of trial and error, so benefit from my many failures."

"I plan on it," she flashed him a smile. "Come sit in the kitchen and I'll put on some coffee."

They settled down for bagels and coffee, sharing idle conversation. Then Jordon's mood turned a little serious.

"I've been having a really hard time, Leo, since Julian,

that's my – was my – husband, since Julian died. I was totally unprepared for Ellie when she arrived. Not with stuff, I had plenty of that, but emotionally, you know?"

"I know what you mean. Thank God, I haven't had to deal with anything major since my wife, Lanie, died. I'm sure I'd be a wreck." The truth was that he'd been a wreck himself over the past few months. First, worried about not finding Baby 13. Now, worried about finding Baby 13.

"Yesterday in the park, well, I was completely out of my mind. I was thinking about leaving Ellie in the park, thinking someone better than me would find her and take care of her."

"Oh, Jeez!" Leo leaned back and put his hands up on his head, as if trying to stop it from exploding.

"I prayed for someone to help me."

He leaned in over the table and grabbed her hand. "Don't ever think that way again, okay?" He was pleading with her.

"I won't. I promise," she reassured him, gently pulling her hand away. "But I wanted you to know how much your help meant to me. And Ellie."

"Jordan, at the risk of looking like a crazy stalker, I want you to know that I will do whatever I can for you and Ellie. Just say the word."

"Well, I'd...," Jordan stumbled over the words, "I'd like to... I'd like it if... Ellie would like it if you came by and checked on us once in a while."

"No problem." Leo answered immediately. "How about every day?"

Jordan smiled. "That would work for us. At least for now."

Leo was wracking his brains trying to figure out what to do next. He'd been over to Jordan's every day for three weeks.

Every time, the medallion reminded him of his mission. Every time, he felt helpless to support this baby Buddha on the road to enlightenment. He realized he needed to find a real Buddhist to see this thing through.

His next step was a visit to The Morning Light Buddhist Temple on 64th St. He'd been by it before but never paid much attention. Now, standing in front of it, he noticed the smaller print on the sign that claimed as practiced in Nepal. That sounded promising. He gingerly opened the door. Instantly the smell of incense brought him back to the monk in the cave, and the temples and villages scattered throughout the deep-cut valleys of the distant mountain range.

"Can I help you?" A monk in dark red robes greeted him with a slight bow, more like a nod of the head, really.

"Ah, I hope so. Is there someone like a director or manager that I can talk to?"

The monk smiled. "Yes. I can get you the senior monk, Brother Guang Wei. Can I tell him the nature of you visit?"

"I'd rather tell him myself if you don't mind."

"Certainly. Please wait here."

Leo was left in a large foyer with a statue of the Buddha, draped with a floral garland, and with a dozen burning candles surrounding it. To the left was a brass bowl with a single stick of incense burning, its smoke making circular patterns as it wafted upward. A large gong covered most of the opposite wall. The entire atmosphere brought back the peacefulness of his time in Nepal. He let out a long breath he wasn't aware he was holding.

The welcoming monk had returned, "Please follow me," he requested, then turned and proceeded down a hallway to the right.

Leo followed the monk past what appeared to be

administrative offices. He was surprised that it all looked like a typical American business setup with modular metal desks, computers and printing stations. The man motioned him into a large office in the back, where an older monk, also in the traditional red robes, was seated.

He got up as Leo entered, and extended his hand, in a western style greeting.

"Hello. I am Brother Guang Wei."

"Nice to meet you sir. My name's Leo DiPalo."

"Mr. DiPalo, how may I help you?"

"It's Leo, please. And I'm not sure if you can. I have a bit of a situation and I'm not sure what to do."

"It sounds curious. Please sit down." He motioned to a chair facing the desk then resumed his seat. "Tell me more."

"It has to do with the tradition of the Thousand Buddhas. I don't pretend to know a lot about it but I met a monk who gave me this." Leo pulled the medallion out of his shirt.

When Brother Quang Wei saw the medallion, his expression changed from politely curious to suspiciously serious.

"Please tell me how you came to have such an item."

It put Leo on the defense. He wasn't sure how much he should say. He settled on his own level of caution. "Let's just say, I was asked to locate someone here in Brooklyn."

"I see," he said as he gracefully but swiftly got up and closed the office door. "And have you?"

"I have."

Brother Quang Wei resumed his seat on the opposite side of the desk. Leo could see excitement light up the old monk's eyes. "And how can I be of help?"

"I'm not sure what to do now."

"So, your obligation is finished. You wish to be free from

further responsibilities." The monk spoke as if it were fact.

"What? No. No way. Not at all." Leo was immediately on the defense, suspicious now himself. "Why would you think that?"

"I'm only drawing a logical conclusion, since you have finished your task."

"My task was to locate and keep safe this child," he corrected.

"Yes. Of course. My misunderstanding. If you wish to participate in the journey from here forward, there are other considerations."

"For instance?"

"The road from here is long and unpredictable. This child could stay here in the city or move anywhere in the world. If you choose to be a part of this story, you must be willing to make whatever adjustments are necessary – for the rest of your life."

"I see. What else?"

"You must be sworn to secrecy. There are those that would like the world to remain the same, to resist the spiritual evolution of humankind and would benefit from control of a such a being."

Leo was shocked. "That sounds ominous. Who could possibly wish ill to a holy being?"

"History is built on such things. The Crucifixion and the martyrdom of saints solidified Roman rule for the next four hundred years. The Crusades and the Spanish Inquisition all helped to solidify Christianity's place of power in the world. The Islamic conquests of the Middle Ages created the largest empire since Rome, encompassing the entire Arabian Peninsula, northern Africa and beyond. The Jewish genocide..."

"Okay. Okay. I get it."

"Those in power fear losing the riches and social standing that they now hold. They, too, are following the trail of Buddhas, but for very different reasons."

Leo took a deep breath. He certainly had not considered any of these implications, but Ellie had stolen his heart completely and, as irrational as it sounded even to him, he knew he would die for her.

"Okay. What else?"

"You must agree to guide the child's spiritual life in whatever tradition the family chooses."

"Really? That's Jewish. How can the Buddha be Jewish?"

"To be Buddha is to live in the transcendent state of oneness with God while also being of this world. It is the next step in the advancement of consciousness, irrelevant to any religious path. When a certain number of people have reached this heightened awareness, the human race will evolve."

"Like one thousand?"

"Yes, but not exactly. Are you familiar with the hypothesis of one hundred monkeys?"

"I can't say I am."

"The idea is that once enough individuals in a society, sometimes called critical mass, believe something, then soon everyone else believes it as well. In our scenario, once enough people have become enlightened, all of humanity evolves into the next level of consciousness, which, presumably is that of light, love and peaceful cooperation. Our tradition holds that the last Buddha will awaken the needed mass."

"So, my job would be to ensure the evolution of the human race?" Leo asked incredulously.

"Yes. Essentially. One piece of it at least. And having a non-Buddhist ally in the community would be an advantage for us, making our involvement less obvious to those watching."

"But who will school Ellie in whatever she needs to know? A Rabbi?"

"Over the hundreds of years, we have placed teachers in all areas of religion and science to cover any eventuality."

"Science? That seems like the antithesis of religion?"

"On the contrary. Science is the basis for religion, the reason religion exists at all. Science takes us to the very edge of understanding, and when it gets there, there are still unanswered questions. Bridging this gap is the purest function of religion."

"Okay, this has all put me over the top, short-circuited my brain."

"It is a lot to consider. We do not need an answer today. I will ask you, however, to leave us the name of this precious individual so that we may make necessary arrangements."

Reluctantly, Leo wrote down the name and address of little Ellie. "I'm going to continue to help this family out." He wanted the monk to know he wasn't going anywhere any time soon.

"We hope you do," the monk nodded. "We thank you." Quang Wei got up and escorted Leo back out to the main doors. "Please come by and visit the temple again."

Leo walked home, not entirely sure what just happened. He resolved to keep a close eye on Jordan and Ellie.

Two days later, Rabbi Amelia Felder knocked on Jordan's door to welcome the new baby to the community and offer any assistance she might need.

Chapter 33

#997

They met outside the church where Devon Johnson was being laid to rest.

"You're looking a little conventional, Brother Chen," Nathan commented, referring to the civilian slacks and sportscoat he had donned for the occasion.

"I wanted to pay my respects without drawing attention away from the family. I thought it best to blend in."

"You look very nice," Kate nodded approval. With his Asian features and his bald head, he still looked a little out of place.

"Thank you and please refer to me simply as Chen for the sake of simplicity."

"Yes. Certainly."

"I've never been to a Christian Funeral service before."

"Me either," Kate responded.

"Really?"

"Yes. My family is Jewish."

"Somehow that reassures me. Is there anything I should know?" They both looked to Nathan.

Nathan thought for a moment. "Nothing special I can think of. Just do what everyone else is doing. I can say that there's a lot of people here. A few hundred at least. Probably because of all the press this thing has gotten. I spotted TV cameras around back." He pointed to a drive alongside the church that led behind the building.

"Is this where the service happens?" Brother Chen asked pointing to the church. "I know there will be an inground burial."

"Yes. The main service is here. They're all a little different so I'm not entirely sure what to expect either. Then we'll probably go to the graveside for a short prayer. Afterward, there will be a reception in the church hall downstairs. We can introduce ourselves to his mother and offer our condolences at that time if we want and then head home."

"Very well. Have you met his mother before?" Brother Chen asked.

"No. She hasn't been around at any of the events. Devon never said much about her. I got the impression she has problems of her own."

"It looks like everyone is going in now," Kate observed. Even in the winter cold, people had been milling around the parking lot. Now they were slowly heading inside.

The church was packed and, as Nathan had suspected, cameras had set up in the back after the service began. It was long and heartbreaking, with each of them fighting off tears. Well, not Kate so much. She gave into them full force, sobbing at times. Nathan and Brother Chen were still pretty much in shock at the loss only they could truly fathom. The odd thing was that their connection had been based on Devon and a shared future vision. Now, there was an awkward silence that hung in the air.

They followed the hearse to the cemetery just a few miles away for a short, and very cold, graveside service then back to the church. Fewer people returned for the reception. The TV cameras were gone

"Hello, Ms. Johnson," Nathan greeted Devon's mother with a gentle handshake. I'm Nathan Morrison. I run an afterschool program Devon was involved with."

"Oh, yes," Ms. Johnson interrupted him. "Yes. Devon told me all about you. Trying to give the city kids a chance..." her voice trailed off for a moment. "I know he was a better boy because of you. Thank you."

"I'm sorry I couldn't do more. He was a nice boy. He wanted to do the right things."

"I'm grateful for all you did for him," she assured him. She turned to Kate, baby obviously due any day. "You keep a close eye on that one," she nodded to Kate's belly. "You can't let them out of your sight. Not for a minute."

"I'm Kate, Nathan's wife. And yes, I'm already worried about her." Kate gave her belly a rub.

"And this is Mr. Chen," Nathan continued with the introductions. "He sponsored the basketball team Devon played on."

"Nice to meet you Mr. Chen." She took his hand. "I've heard about you too. You know, Devon hated basketball. He only played because he liked you. He said you always wore red big robes." She waved her hands down her body indicating the flowing cloth. "Aren't you a monk or something?"

"Yes. I thought that for today, I would be less obvious, out of respect for you and your family."

"I appreciate that. Be sure to stay for refreshments."

"Yes, thank you," Nathan replied. They walked slowly out among the remaining family and friends, heading for the door.

"Brother Chen, will we see you again?" It was Nathan asking.

"As far as I know, I will be staying at the center for the time being. You are welcome to visit any time. Perhaps we will continue to sponsor a basketball team if your program continues next year."

"Maybe. I haven't even thought that far ahead."

Kate added quickly, "In any event, I'm sure we'll keep in touch."

They parted company in the parking lot, heading to their cars.

They were on the way home from the funeral when Kate grabbed her belly and leaned forward.

"What's wrong?" Nathan's head swiveled from his wife to traffic, concern evident in his voice.

Kate gasped. "My water just broke. Looks like we're having a baby." Joy collided head-on with the heavy sadness of a moment ago, like two freight trains. Nathan didn't know how he felt at that moment. He went into autopilot.

"Okay. Okay. I got this."

"I hope so," Kate replied through clenched teeth as the first contraction set in. "You drive. I'll call the doctor."

Nathan sped toward home to begin the waiting. The easy chair had been set up with comfy pillows, an ice bucket and a stop watch for timing contractions.

Kate went into another contraction almost immediately.

"Are you okay? What's up? I thought they would start slow, you know, don't go to the hospital until they were five minutes apart?" Nathan had memorized the process.

"That's what I thought too, honey. We read the same books. Remember?" Kate was still clenching her teeth.

"Yeah. So, what's going on here?"

"Well, if I had to guess, I'd say the baby didn't read the books. I think she's ready now."

"What do you mean now! Like NOW now?"

Kate sucked in another breath. "Yeah," she forced out. "NOW now."

Nathan made an illegal U-turn to redirect them to Swedish Covenant Hospital.

"Hey," Kate admonished him. "If we get pulled over, it takes fifteen minutes to get a ticket!"

"Right. Sorry. How do you know these things?"

"In this case, from experience." Kate was catching her breath.

"Oh. Why am I not surprised?"

"I've gotten much better,"

"I hope so. You'll be driving our daughter around."

"Says the guy who just pulled an illegal U-turn." Teeth clenched again.

"Right. I'm okay. I got this." Nathan reassured both of them.

They'd packed the Go bag in the car two weeks ago, just in case, and set up as much as they could ahead of time. They'd even executed a dry run through admissions to avoid problems or delays when the time came. All that went out the window when they pulled up to the ER doors. Nathan had always heard that heart patients got top priority in the ER. Apparently, the rule applies to pregnant women, too.

They were admitted immediately and whisked up to the maternity ward. Now, they were set up in a comfortable birthing room. The doctor had come in immediately, checked Kate over, then told them to settle in

"Everything looks okay. It might be two hours or so. Hard to say," he declared nonchalantly.

"Wait. What happened to the hours sitting at home waiting? Timing contractions, chewing ice?" Nathan had demanded. "Are you sure she's okay?"

"She's fine Mr. Morrison. Sometimes it just doesn't go that way." He shrugged his shoulders as he left the room.

The doctor turned out to be exactly right. It was two hours later when he returned to the room. Kate was exhausted. Nathan never left her side. He hated to see her in so much pain and couldn't wait for it to be over. He couldn't imagine how Kate must feel. The doctor was considering a C section when things finally came into the home stretch.

As if calling out sports plays, the doctor narrated her progress.

"I see her head. You're doing great. Keep pushing. Hard!"

"Fuck you." Kate blurted out as she pushed. "I am pushing." Then, in a moment of clarity, she added, "Oops. Sorry."

"No problem," the doctor laughed. "That's it. Her head is out. Now her shoulders and now, here she is." Kate felt an enormous physical relief, finally letting go of Nathan's hand which was by now red and swollen. Nathan also finally let go a deep breath. As he heard his baby girl cry for the first time, he felt an overwhelming sense of love, like his whole body was shaking. When the doctor laid little Naomi on Kate's chest, Nathan thought his own chest would bust open. Then he froze. He grabbed his chest. Kate freaked out.

"Nathan! What's wrong?"

Nathan was speechless. He grabbed Kate's hand and held it to his chest. Underneath the hospital garb, Kate could clearly feel the vibration of Nathan's medallion. They locked eyes, unable to speak.

"Is everything okay?" the nurse was asking. After she got no response, she asked again with concern. "Are you two okay?"

Realizing they were upsetting the nurse, they shook it off as best they could.

"Yes, fine," Nathan assured her. Kate nodded, speechless.

Deep in a cave in the Himalayas, a monk was aroused out of his meditation. He rose, crossed to the wall opposite him, and, with a piece of charcoal, drew one line vertically on the wall, leaving three lines uncrossed.

Chapter 34

#998

Chris and Marion Rivera were having their long-awaited christening for their infant son, James. They were glad they had waited until the first of the year to give everyone an opportunity to attend unpressured by to-do lists.

As Chris and Marion donned their Sunday-best church cloths, Sarah was trying to keep James in the cutest little white oxford shoes she had ever seen. As soon as she got them on and turned her back, they were off again. It had become a game for James but a bit frustrating for Sarah. Still, she couldn't help giggling along with him. She lifted him up in his tiny white suit that would soon be draped over by a lacey flowing gown for the church service. Relenting for the moment, she headed downstairs with James, shoes in hand.

"Oh my God, Sarah. You're amazing. He looks absolutely irresistible." Marion swooped James up in the air, causing him to squeal with laughter.

Chris, noticing the shoes, held his hand out to Sarah. "He

really hates them, doesn't he?"

Sarah laughed. "You might keep them on for a few pictures. Luckily, he doesn't mind those so much." She was referring to the little white socks remaining on James' feet. "From far away, they'll look like shoes."

"Good point," Chris agreed. "So, shall we go?" he asked Marion.

The christening went off without incident, but the whole time, Sarah was uneasy. How was James going to get proper training as a Catholic? Why hadn't Father Rico said anything to the Riveras about James birthright? The monk hadn't actually said what would happen once she found the baby. She had assumed finding him would be the hard part. Now, she realized, she was wrong.

The next morning, Sarah knocked politely on the door to the rectory office.

"Come in," Father Rico called out.

"Good morning, Father." She entered timidly, wringing her hands.

"Hello, Sarah. What can I do for you?"

"I'm wondering about James."

"Yes?"

"When are we going to tell Marion and Chris that their baby is the next Buddha?"

"We're not."

"What? Why not? Shouldn't they know?" She started pacing nervously.

"Sarah, please sit down." Father Rico motioned to the couch in his office. Once she was settled, he looked directly at her. "It is our responsibility to provide the best environment possible for James."

"Yes. But -"

"And that, as best I see it, is to allow him to be raised in the loving supportive household of his birth. If that changes or if James becomes endangered in some way, decisions might need to be made otherwise, but for now, things will remain as is."

"What do you mean? How will James get everything he needs? Who will teach him?"

"I will."

"But you're not Buddhist?"

"No, I'm not. Enlightenment is not religion specific. All paths lead to God."

"Shouldn't we do something?"

"The fulfillment of the prophecy is for mankind to evolve into its own greatness, without intervention. We have already intervened in a small way by identifying James and creating a situation for him to flourish safely. But we can't want enlightenment for him. He has to want it for himself."

"But Marion and Chris have a right to know."

"So they can do what? There is no good that comes from the telling. At this point, it will only elicit feelings of betrayal and likely get us both thrown out of his life."

Sarah winced at the possibility. "But you're asking me to lie to them."

Father Rico considered the omission isn't really lying tact but knew that was, in itself, a lie.

"Yes. Or take yourself out of the equation."

"What!" Sarah was stunned. "Leave James? Now?"

"It's an option. You have fulfilled the monk's request. You have no further obligation."

"No way! Not happening."

"If you choose to stay, then I ask that you respect the

decisions of those who have been following this prophecy for two thousand years."

"Yes. I suppose so," Sarah conceded.

Father Rico was not convinced. "We can continue to have conversations about this. In the meantime, can I count on your discretion?"

"Yes. And thank you, Father." She hesitated. "So, for now, we stay here?"

"It's possible Mr. Rivera will get transferred to a small town in Montana."

"What?"

"It's in everyone best interest that he take it."

"How do you know that?"

"We have been planning for this moment for two thousand years, Sarah."

"Right."

Sarah didn't have it in her to ask any more questions. Her head was already swimming.

Chapter 35

#999

Leo stopped by every morning to visit Ellie and Jordon, bringing the usual bagels and lox. And every morning Jordan put on coffee around 9:30. Today, Jordan had put in a special order for an extra bagel saying, "There's someone I want you to meet."

When Leo arrived, there was a middle-aged woman sitting at the table drinking coffee with Jordan. Leo immediately assumed it was a relative so he was taken aback when Jordan introduced her as Rabbi Amelia Felder.

"She was just assigned to the synagogue around the corner. She came by yesterday to say hello."

Leo immediately became concerned about this new player. What would happen when the Teacher arrived? Would there be any problems?

"When I told her about you, she wanted to meet you, to make sure you're not a creepy stalker."

"Jordan! I never said that, in so many words, but…," she

turned to Leo, "you can't be too careful nowadays. No offense, unless you are a stalker in which case, take great offense."

"None taken," Leo waved his hand. "Jordan and I have talked about how crazy this whole thing has been. But we really seem to hit it off. And, of course, you've met Ellie."

"Have I ever. Have you ever seen such a perfect child?"

"That's exactly what I said," Leo agreed.

"Oh, stop, you two," Jordan finally got a word in. "She's just like any other baby."

Both Rabbi Amelia and Leo responded simultaneously, "No, she's not." They turned to look at each other, Leo somewhat suspiciously.

"Well, that's something you two agree on, then. How nice." Jordan smiled at them both. "How about we eat?"

Leo emptied the contents of the bag onto plates that were already set out on the table. Jordan poured coffee and they all sat down to get to know each other.

"So, Leo, you travel much?" Rabbi Amelia asked.

"Not really. Up until recently, I've had a full-time job that kept me pretty busy."

"Really? Well, you should get out more if you can. The world is such an amazing place. I just got back from Nepal."

Leo dropped his bagel. "What?"

"Yes. There's nothing like a lovely walk in the Himalayas to clear your head."

"Leo, you told me you were there just this summer," Jordan said.

"Yes. I, uh, took a leave of absence from work when my wife died." Leo was trying to catch up. He retrieved his bagel which, thankfully, had landed on his plate, lox and cheese side down. "It was quite a journey. Changed my life."

Just then, Ellie let out a chirp from the baby monitor on the counter. "Excuse me. I'll be right back." Jordan got up and headed into the bedroom.

"So, Leo," Rabbi Amelia said in a hushed tone, "I know the monk sent you. I just want you to know I know and we're doing okay. Not to worry."

"Ah, who's we?" Leo was not about to be cut out of this story.

"You and me. No worries. And a few others, you know, in the background."

"Just so you're clear, I'm not going anywhere." Leo looked her sternly in the eye.

"I wouldn't hear of it. And neither would Jordan. She thinks the world of you."

"Have you told her? About the baby?"

"No, and I don't plan on it."

"What do you mean, you're not planning on it?"

"For starters, she won't believe us. She'll feel angry and betrayed and kick us out of her life, or worse."

Leo's heart sank. "What could be worse?" It was more rhetorical than an actual question.

"She calls the police and accuses us of some terrible crime we are innocent of."

Leo looked up at the Rabbi. He knew she was right. He was in too far. Telling her now wouldn't be good for anyone. This is a secret he might take to his grave. If he was to stay with this family, as the monk had warned him, it would have to be forever.

"What do we do in the meantime?"

"We love them and protect them as best we can."

"I can do that. Heck, I already am."

"There's a lovely town in Montana that might be a perfect

spot."

Just then Jordan came out of the bedroom with a blanket draped over her shoulder, baby Ellie tucked underneath, nursing.

"So, I guess you could say my prayers have been answered," she said. "The two things I asked for, a good friend and a good Rabbi, are sitting at my table, having coffee. Life is getting better all the time."

"Yes, it is," they all agreed.

Chapter 36

#1000

Nathan called Brother Chen as soon as they got home from the hospital.

"Hello, Brother Chen. I just wanted to let you know that Kate had our baby two days ago."

"Congratulations. A girl, isn't it?"

"Yes. And she is an absolute miracle. You have to come over to meet her."

"Yes. Certainly, but I'm very busy with things here. I'm not sure when I can come."

"No. You really have to come over. She is the perfect little Buddha baby."

Brother Chen hesitated at the reference. He did not want to ask the next question over the phone. "Yes. Of course she is. How about tomorrow afternoon?"

"That would be perfect. I'll text you the address."

Nathan greeted Brother Chen at the door. "Come in,

please. Kate is in the back resting with the baby, Naomi Christine."

"Wonderful. And everyone is well?"

"Yes. Perfectly healthy."

"And…" Brother Chen left the question unasked.

"It appears we have been blessed with the last Buddha."

"Are you sure?"

"Quite sure. Kate felt the medallion, too."

"And how are you doing with that information?"

What had started out as bliss and joy, had spiraled for Nathan into fear and self-doubt. All he could think about was how he had failed Devon. How was he going to keep his own daughter safe? What if he failed again?

"To be honest, I'm making myself a little crazy. I'm still trying to reconcile Devon's death with this whole picture. What did I do wrong? What do I have to do differently now?"

"What is most important is the child's safety. If you feel Chicago is not the best place for her, you should consider other options."

"What do you think?" He desperately wanted Brother Chen to have the answers.

"Each of us must do what we think is best. You are fortunate. Your options are almost unlimited."

"What do you mean?"

"You can stay here if you like, or move anywhere you like. I, or someone like me, will be wherever you are."

"Chicago no longer feels safe for me, or for Kate. We're wondering if Nepal is best?"

"It is best to raise the child in a culture you are both familiar with. It will be easier for everyone."

"I don't know where to go!" Nathan hung his head in frustration.

"Have you considered Montana?"

Nathan looked up. He remembered the conversation with Kate last year. It seemed like a lifetime ago. "The Garden of 1,000 Buddhas."

"Yes. You are familiar?"

"Kate found it online when I first got back from Nepal."

"A small town. Very safe. You can still see family. You can find work. The monastery is there."

"Yes," Nathan agreed. "Yes, I can see that being a solution. Will you come with us?"

"That is not for me to decide."

Epilogue

A monk, a Rabbi and a Priest enter a cave deep in the Himalayan mountains. Placing their packs gently on the cave floor, they head into the inner sanctum where a monk chants softly.

As they enter, each prostrates fully before the monk, then takes a seat on blankets set out on the floor.

"Brother Chen, tell me of the Chicago situation?" The monk nodded in Chen's direction.

"Nathan, Kate and Naomi are headed to Montana as soon as they can find housing and work."

"And you will accompany them?"

"If it is your wish."

"It is my wish." He turned to Rabbi Amelia. "And you, Sister Amelia. Tell me about New York."

"They're safe for the moment. I am hoping to initiate a move to Montana within the year. I assume Leo will go with them. It might even be more conducive if Leo had a job offer there. He's become quite attached to the family."

"And will you accompany them?"

"If you wish, Master."

"I do." He then turned to Father Rico. "Brother Rico. Tell me first about Brother Bensi."

"Unfortunately, we could not save him."

"Do we know what damage he has caused?"

"It is unclear, but we believe Green Dragon is now involved."

"This is very serious. And the situation in Guam?"

"A work transfer is being processed for Chris Rivera. He doesn't have to take it. Sarah and I will do what we can to encourage it."

"You will travel with them?"

"If you wish. And Sarah would like to go as well."

"Make it so."

About the Story

While I was traveling through Montana on business in April of 2018, I was looking for botanical gardens. It was one of the ways I spent my free time while I was on the road. That's when I happened across a remote garden called Garden of 1000 Buddhas. The vegetation was still just poking through from the Spring thaw so there weren't a lot of plantings. Still, it was an impressive place with, as promised, 1000 statues of the Buddha. In addition to the fascinating gardens, the site also houses a retreat and teaching center. Ever since then, this story has been brewing in my imagination. Here's their website. https://www.ewam.org/centers/ewam-usa

About the Author

Marie LeClaire has spent the past thirty years as a mental health counselor encouraging others to look beyond our sometimes-limited perspective and see a bigger picture of what influences our lives and guides our behavior. She has been writing novels and short stories for the past five years. She still does a little counseling part time, but her love now is purely fiction - sort of. After all, art imitates life, doesn't it? After wandering around much of her adult life, she currently calls Worcester, MA home. Read some of her stories on her website MLeClaire.com

Other Books by Marie LeClaire

The Last Yard Sale

Four Bewitched items change everything.

A Soldier's Last Mission

A fallen soldier reaches out from beyond the grave to save his son's life.

The Old Wool Factory

When Gabby is let in on the family secret, she soon learns that what she thinks becomes real,
-and intention is everything.

The Mistaken Haunting of Seth Harrison

Lizzie Borden took an axe.
Gave her mother forty whacks.

But did she?
Three grifters get caught up in the Lizzie Borden murders and it plays itself out one hundred years later.

Made in the USA
Middletown, DE
23 May 2023